Besotted

Georgia Le Carre

Editor: http://www.loriheaford.com/
Proofreader:
http://nicolarhead.wix.com/proofreadingservices

Besotted

(Book 3 of The Billionaire Banker series)

Published by Georgia Le Carre

ISBN: 978-0-9928249-5-2

You can discover more information about Georgia Le Carre and future releases here.

https://www.facebook.com/georgia.lecarre

https://twitter.com/georgiaLeCarre

http://www.goodreads.com/GeorgiaLeCarre

The way to make money is to buy when blood is running in the street.

John D. Rockefeller

Table of Contents

Blake Law Barrington

April, 2014

The knock on the Lanesborough Suite's door is firm and unhesitant. I glance at my watch. Very punctual. I like that. I open the door and... My, my, she is a beauty: waist-length, straight blonde hair, gorgeous big eyes. And scarlet lips. Lana almost never colors her lips so red. A pity. She is wearing a long, white coat belted at the waist and really, really high heels. They remind me of the shoes Lana wore the first night I met her.

She is chewing gum, though. I hate that. She must watch too many movies about big-hearted hookers. I put my hand out, palm outstretched. For a moment she looks at me, clueless. I raise my eyebrows and she hurriedly takes the gum out of her mouth and drops it into my hand. Then she raises her own eyebrows and cheekily stretches her hand out.

'Don't you want to come in first?' I ask, amused but not showing it.

'Of course,' she says and walks past me. Her accent is odd. She must be making it up as she goes along.

I close the door and watch her walk ahead of me. She has a good walk. I like a woman who can walk with grace. She stops in front of the low table where there is a platter of fresh fruit and a bottle of champagne cooling in an ice bucket, and turns around to face me. For a moment I am distracted by the picture she makes standing in the agreeably English decor of traditional prints and chintzes teamed with bold choices of acid greens and Schiaparelli pinks. I put the gum on the sideboard.

'I'm sorry, what's your name?'

'Rumor.'

I smile. The name suits her. She looks like a rumor. Couldn't possibly be true.

'Would you like a glass of champagne?'

She lifts one foot and lets it swing back. It is impossibly erotic. 'I'd like to be paid first.'

I don't react to the provocation. 'The money is by the lamp.'

She glances at the neat pile of money as she works the two buttons on her coat. The coat lands on the sofa behind her. She is wearing a very short white dress. Wordlessly, she turns away from me and bends from the waist, so her ass is pushed out and her skirt rides up to where her smooth thighs indent and I glimpse the other thing I had specified—a freshly waxed pussy. The lips are already swollen and reddened, and as I watch moisture starts to gather.

Immediately I am hard as hell.

Slowly, holding that position, she counts the money. The desire to ram her while she is

counting her money is strong, but I resist. She puts the last note on top of the pile she has counted, and turns to face me.

'All there?'

'Yeah,' she says slowly, her acquired accent undergoing another change. 'All there.'

I move towards her and put my hand between her legs. Obligingly, she parts them and my fingers start to play with the soaking flesh.

'So Rumor, what shall we do with you?'

'Mr. Barrington—'

'Blake,' I say persuasively, as I continue to explore the silky, wet folds.

She takes a steadying breath. 'Blake, we can do anything you want to do, so long as you remember anything kinky is extra.'

'What kind of kinky things are on offer?' I plunge my middle finger into her.

She gasps and sinks her teeth into her bottom lip. I watch with amusement.

'You're the customer. Tell me what kinky things you want and I'll do them.'

'Have you been on many callouts?'

'Not really. Just one other time.'

'Tell me—what did he do to you?'

'He fucked me really hard.'

'How hard?'

'So hard I was too sore to go to my next appointment.'

'Have you got another appointment after this?'

'No.'

'Good.'

She turns around, lifts the heavy curtain of golden hair and offers me her zip. I pull it down and she wriggles out of her dress. It falls on the pink carpet. I run my hand along the nude flesh. She shivers. I turn her around to face me. Her body is very beautiful and her pupils are so dilated that her irises are almost black. I lift her up—she is as light as a feather—and carry her into the lavish, blue bedroom. I lay her down gently on the king-sized, four-poster bed. I look down on her pale body. I have bought her. For the next hour she is mine to do anything I please with. The thought electrifies me.

'Open your legs,' I command.

Immediately she lifts her knees and lets them fall open so her swollen reddened sex is exposed to me. I have one hour to fuck, and that is exactly what I do. I fuck her until she is panting, her slim young body slipping against mine. Until she screams. She lies on her back, her eyes closed.

I cup her breast in the palm of my hand. It fits perfectly. 'That was great. Thanks.'

She sits up. I watch the curve her waist and hips make and I feel like pulling her down and having her all over again, but I have an appointment in less than thirty minutes. She goes into the bathroom.

'Don't wash,' I tell her.

She says nothing. Just nods.

I hear water running. By the time she comes out I am already fully dressed.

'I'll book you again next week,' I tell her.

'Sure. Arrange it with the agency.' She seems oddly shy.

'OK.'

'I need to use the toilet.'

By the time I come out she is fully dressed and waiting in the sitting room.

'Do you need a ride back? The hotel offers a complimentary chauffeur-driven Rolls-Royce.'

She shakes her head.

A thought. She is wearing nothing under the dress. 'Lift your dress.'

She doesn't appear surprised, just quietly parts her coat and lifts her dress, and exposes her sex to me. My seed is still leaking out of her. I walk up to her, gently cup her buttocks and drop to my knees. I look up at her. She is watching me curiously. Bending my head I lick her slit, puffy with engorged, glistening flesh. She moans. I could have her again if I wanted to. I pull her dress back down and walk her to the door.

'See you then,' she calls.

I close the door and go to stand at the triple-glazed, floor to ceiling window. It has a marvelous view of Wellington Arch. I look at my watch and I catch sight of the pile of money sitting on the low table. I pick it up and put it into my jacket pocket, then I take my mobile out, and call her.

'You forgot your money.'

She laughs. 'Give it to me tonight,' she says.

'You're spoiling my fantasy,' I tell her.

'Oh yeah?' Her voice is challenging, full of life.

'Yeah, but nice touch—the blonde wig.'

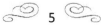 5

'Thought you might like a change.'

'I love you.'

'I love you too,' she says softly. I imagine her sitting in the back of the Bentley.

'Text me when you get home.'

'I will.'

She makes a kissing sound and then she is gone.

I look at my watch. Ten minutes left before my next appointment with the Crown Prince Muqrin Bin Abdel-Aziz of the House of Saud. I ring the twenty-hour butler service and ask them to summon housekeeping. The Head Butler, Daniel Jordan arrives in less than five minutes with three foreign-looking chambermaids in tow.

In two minutes they have put right the bed and bathroom and out of the door, smiling broadly, their tips snug inside their tight fists. Daniel discreetly removes the gum from the sideboard, and perfumes the air with attar of roses. Afterwards, he takes up his position in the dining room, which is actually my favorite part of this particular suite. Soon food arrives on trolleys and waiters start gathering in the kitchen. Laura calls—His Highness and his entourage are in the lobby and on their way up. The butler starts walking towards the door.

I shoot my cuffs.

October, 2013

We build our temples for tomorrow,
strong as we know how,
And we stand on top of the mountain,
free within ourselves.

Langston Hughes

One

Lana Bloom

When I come back from the church, Blake is awake. He must have heard the car in the driveway. He is standing in the living room waiting for me. There are bluish shadows under his eyes, which make his eyes seem as if the entire sky has been boiled down and rendered in those two small points. He smiles faintly, like he does not quite know how to react to me, and my heart breaks for him. I remember reading George Orwell: *You wear a mask and your face grows to fit it.*

I go up to him and lay my cheek on his chest. He has had a shower and he smells clean and fresh. Like my idea of heaven. I feel him nuzzle my hair. It is like a prayer for which there are no words, and my love increases and ripens, the way fruit does in the autumn. He will never again have to pretend to be anything he is not. Or wear his mask with me. I think of Beauty dancing in the great ballroom with Beast. I am madly in love with Beast.

'I woke up and found you gone,' he said. His voice is different, softer.

'Did you think I'd run away?'

'You can never run away from me, Lana. I would journey into the underworld to find you. You are mine.'

'I went to church.'

'Yes, Brian said. I thought you didn't believe in God.'

I look up at him. He is heartbreak in a shallow basket. 'For short there is tall, for sad there is happy. For dark there must be light. I wanted to align myself with the God of goodness. I wanted to ask his help.'

'Oh, Lana. You and all the believers of this world. You pray and you pray and all your billions of unanswered prayers are like wailing cries somewhere. Your God doesn't exist.' His voice is so sad.

'How do you know?'

'Because if he did the world wouldn't be the way it is. And even if he does exist he is definitely not the lord of this world.'

I look up into his face. Already the weight of being the head of the Barrington dynasty is changing the shape of his face.

'Why do you say that?'

'Look around you, Lana. The entire planet— land, air and sea—has been poisoned by sheer greed, your food is toxic, you are governed by

sociopaths who wage war after war with impunity while promising peace, and humanity itself is poised on the brink of extinction. Who do you think is in charge? Your God of love and light, or mine?'

There is a tap on the door. Blake closes his eyes and sighs. 'Maybe this conversation can wait till later,' he says. He looks so tired, so burdened, I wish I could take him away from all this.

I nod and move out of the circle of his arms.

'Come in,' he calls. And I see the transformation in him—the way the mask of power slips back into place—and lament it. Vulnerability has no place in the world of gaudy wealth.

By the time Brian opens the door and comes in the mask is firmly in place. The man who had nuzzled my hair has dissolved.

'Your brother is on the line.'

'Marcus?'

'No, Quinn.'

I notice the look of surprise on his face. He takes the phone and Brian leaves, closing the door behind him.

'Quinn. Yes. No. You will come? Three thirty p.m. Of course, they'll be there. But you have nothing to fear, I will be there.' I feel the strength flow back into his voice. 'While I am alive they can do nothing. Have you spoken to Marcus? You should call him. This has affected him greatly. He was very close to...Dad. When will you come? Good I'll send someone to pick you up. Goodbye Quinn.'

He ends the call and looks at me. 'If ever anything happens to me, the only one you must trust is Quinn.'

Fear like I have never known slams into me. And a pain takes root so deep inside myself that I find myself gasping the next breath. 'Why do you say that? Are you in danger?'

'I don't think so, but it is always wise to be safe. I have made extensive plans to protect you and Sorab in the event anything does happen to me. You will be safe. You will have money and a new identity.'

I gaze at him in horror. At that moment he becomes my greatest enemy. Money? Is he mad? 'Fuck you!' I scream suddenly. 'Extensive plans to protect me and Sorab? If you die on me I don't want a fucking penny from you. It's blood money.'

He strides towards me and crushes me tightly against his broad chest. I crumple inside his arms. 'Nothing is going to happen to me. I just said that as a precaution. The way other people take out life insurance.'

'You are my angel,' I sob. 'I cannot go on without you.'

'I cannot lie to you, Lana. If I have to I will sacrifice myself for you, over and over. But you must be strong. You have Sorab.'

'Has it become hot in here?' I feel feverish, as if I could faint.

Immediately he tilts my face up to his. 'You're pale.'

'No kidding,' I say, but my voice seems to come from far away. My eyes burn.

'I'm not trying to scare you, Lana. I'm trying to make you feel safe. I could die tomorrow in a car accident. I want you and Sorab to be safe and well. That's all.'

'Fuck you.' I wish I could wrap my arms around him and tell him not to go anywhere.

'Stay here. I'll go get something—'

'No, no, you won't come back. Don't leave me, please.'

'It's OK, OK. I'm not going anywhere.'

There is a sound from below. We both turn to look at him. He gazes back at us with large, curious eyes and for an instant, for a disconcerting instant, it is as if he can see through us, right through to our tormented souls. Blake releases me and goes to his son. Sorab makes a shrill sound of delight as he picks him up. The child lays both his hands flat on his father's cheeks as if he is trying to get all his attention. And when his father nods, he laughs. His father throws him up into the air and catches him while he laughs uproariously.

Oh God, oh God. If only he was just a normal person, if we could just live a normal life, but here he is. Trying to be normal. Trying his best to give us all he can. Yes, I do not know him. There is much left to be done, but this, this can be the prelude to our life. For I am determined to be there each morning when his eyes flutter open.

 13

Two

Sorab and I leave after breakfast with Tom. Blake kisses us goodbye. He will not be coming with us. He will be going the way he came, in a black hawk. I tell Tom to stop by Billie's. Then I call her.

'Are you all right?' she asks me urgently.
'We're fine. We're on our way to you.'
'Who's we?'
'Sorab and me.'
'How long before you get here?'
'Two hours.'
'I'll be waiting for you,' she says, and ends the call abruptly. I look at the phone in my hand with surprise. Strange. I thought she might want to chat, find out more. Oh well.

I knock on her door and it is suddenly flung open. Billie snatches Sorab out of my startled hands and runs with him towards the room Billie and I have together decorated as Sorab's. Slightly bewildered, I close the front door and follow them. I walk into the blue and yellow room in time to see her

14

deposit Sorab in his cot, shove a toy into his hands, and turn towards me with a contorted face.

'What?' I ask and she launches herself at me. She hugs me so tight I can hardly breathe.

'Hey,' I say. 'It's going to be OK.'

That only makes her go stiff in my arms. She pulls away from me. 'Don't lie to me, please.'

I stare at her. I am speechless with shock. Even though her voice is utterly normal, tears are escaping from her eyes and running quickly down her face.

'It's never going to be OK, is it?'

'Of course it is.'

'No, it's not,' she mutters darkly.

I open and close my mouth without having said anything. I have never seen Billie like this before. It shocks me. She's always so cool, so sarcastic.

'The old rat's dead. You're not going to tell me *that* was an accident.'

I shake my head slowly.

'See,' she says, fresh tears slipping down her cheeks.

'Yes, but it is over now.'

'Over? Can't you see that it will never be "over"? I wish to God you had never gone into that fucked up family of reptiles.'

I grip her by her arms. 'But I did, Bill. I'm in it. I love Blake with all my heart. And he is Sorab's father.' I turn and look at my son. He is gazing at us again with those big, innocent eyes; not crying, not upset, but aware that something is not right.

 15

'Have you chosen wisely?'

For a moment the words are like thorns in my heart. I close my eyes. Then I open them and face Billie. 'I cannot be without him, Bill. I simply can't.'

Billie wipes her nose on the sleeve of her oversized T-shirt.

'Let me go get you some tissue.'

'You can't. I ran out yesterday.'

'Oh, Bill! Wait here.'

I go into her bathroom and tear off some toilet paper. When I go back to the room she is standing exactly where I left her. I fold the toilet paper, clip it around her nose, and say, 'Blow.'

She cracks a smile, takes the toilet paper from me, and blows her nose noisily. 'I've been so frightened and confused these last few days.'

'Come on, let's discuss this over a cup of tea,' I cajole.

'All right,' she agrees and reaching into the cot picks Sorab up. Together we go to the kitchen. She closes the door and puts Sorab on the ground. Immediately he starts crawling very fast across the floor.

'My God look at him go,' Billie exclaims, for the moment her earlier worries forgotten.

I laugh. 'He changes from day to day. Sometimes I wake up in the morning and I swear he has grown in the night.'

I fill the kettle with water while Billie lays a plastic mat on the floor and throws some toys on it. Sorab squeals and moves quickly towards them. While Billie sets about preparing Sorab's milk, I

drop tea bags into two mugs and three-quarter fill them with boiling water. I look into the cupboard where the biscuits are usually kept and it is empty. I open the fridge and peer into its impressive bareness.

'Want some milkie, banker baby?' I hear Billie ask Sorab.

Sorab lifts both hands and waves them in the air.

'Good baby,' she praises, and, gently pushing him down to the plastic mat, puts the teat into his mouth. She holds the bottle in place with one finger until he grasps it with both hands.

'Don't you have any food at all in this house?'

Billie gets off the floor and turns towards me. 'Nope,' she replies, totally unconcerned.

'Want some of Sorab's grape biscuits?'

'OK.'

I shake out a couple and we sit next to each other.

I watch her put six spoons of sugar into her tea and stir it morosely. She takes a sip. 'Well?'

I tell her everything I know.

She frowns. 'It's all a bit hard to believe, isn't it?'

'I'm sure it was far more difficult for the people who thought the world was flat to accept that it was actually round. Wouldn't people on the bottom half be falling off? But the world is round. From young we have been trained to unquestionably accept what we are told from our parents and teachers. They taught it to us just as they had learned it. What if they, too, had been deliberately taught the wrong thing?'

'OK, I get that they want to cull the 'useless eaters'. I even get that they start wars not because they are promoting democracy and freedom, but because they want the country's oil or gold or whatever. But why are they poisoning the land, water and air? Don't they have to breathe the same air and live on the same land as us?'

'I don't have the answers, but I intend to find out.'

'What really worries me is how safe are you?'

I sigh. 'I haven't really had a chance to speak to Blake about many things, but one thing I do know is that if Sorab and I were not safe now, I wouldn't be here talking to you.'

'So is Blake the new head of the Barrington empire now?'

'I guess so.'

'What about his older brother? Shouldn't he be the next in line? And if he isn't, wouldn't he be jealous and plotting Blake's downfall?'

I cover my eyes. 'I don't have any answers, Bill. I am scared. The future frightens me, but Blake is nobody's fool. He plays his cards very close to his chest. He never once let on that he knew his father was watching. He let it all unfold in precisely the manner he had decided it would.'

Three

I know that Blake will be home very late because there is so much for him to organize. Even while I was with him the phone calls never stopped. As I promised to do, I call him when we reach the apartment building. We don't talk for long—he is busy. I put my key through the door and realize that this is now home for me. It is where I live with my little family.

So much has happened here.

I play for a while with Sorab, then feed him and put him to bed. I prepare some food—grilled cheese on toast, and, eat it alone—I clean up after myself and wander about the place. From room to room I go switching on lights. It all feels so still and silent. Tonight I cannot bear any shadows. I see ghosts everywhere. I wish Blake would come home. When the phone rings I grab it with relief.

'Hello.'

'Hello, my darling. I'm missing you.' His voice is like velvet in my ear.

'Me too.'

'What are you doing?'

'Nothing. When are you coming home?'

I feel almost tearful. So much has happened that I do not understand. My head is so full of questions and worries. We haven't made love since that night at the Ritz, and I long to feel him on my skin, and deep inside me. I am desperate to forget, to purr, to lose myself and ride that wave of ecstasy. I decide to have a bath, a really long bath, with bubbles and scented oils. I lay my head back and try to relax.

Everything will work out.

Everything *will* work out.

But I am unable to relax. I get out of the bath, dry myself down, lather my skin with some lotion that has honey and extracts of avocado in and lie on the bed reading. By ten Blake is still not home. I go to the fridge and pour myself a glass of white wine. I should put some music on. It feels so deserted and strange. I check on Sorab. All is fine there.

I stand for a while in the balcony. For some reason I think of Jack. Ever since that last time I saw him I have not heard from him. I wonder where he is and what he is up to. I look up to the stars and say a silent prayer for him. Wherever you are, be well. The night air is cold and makes me shiver. Eventually I return to the bed and my book. I want to wait up for Blake, but I fall asleep while reading.

Something wakes me. He is home. I see the glow of the little moon-face lamp under Sorab's door. Softly, I open the door and freeze in the doorway. Blake is standing by the cot staring at Sorab as he

sleeps. His hands are gripping the cot so hard, his knuckles show white. He has opened a window and the night outside has become coal black. No stars. No moon. A soft breeze blows in. I feel it on the bare skin of my arms. Goosebumps scatter. The room is full of clinging shadows. My heart hitches.

He whips his head around suddenly, and I am face to face with him. I see his eyes. For a moment it is as if he does not recognize me. I do not recognize him. It must be my imagination in overdrive but it is as if I have interrupted a powerful predator. His eyes burn through me, angry blue.

'I regret nothing I would do it all again in a heartbeat, if I had to,' he whispers. The sound is fierce and heady with male dominance.

We are locked in a stare, neither of us blinking.

I am mesmerized by his gaze. Here is the man who has a hold on me, on my soul. And he has the keys to secret rooms I have yet to open. They are full of dark secrets. I am scared. Scared for us. Scared that the secrets will defeat me. That he will not give me the keys. The breath catches in my throat. My heart skips a beat. My head is flooded with so many unanswered questions.

He makes a sound, husky, unintelligible.

And suddenly he is beautiful beyond anything I have seen. He is my man. Mine forever. I love him. I open my mouth and words flow from my heart.

'I know our lives will never be the same again. I know you are trapped in a world that is like nothing I have ever known, but I am willing to climb mountains, cross rivers, and travel barefoot over thorns and rocks if it takes me to you. I will find you. I promise,' I whisper.

'I hope you never find me in the place where I exist, Lana.' The words are ripped out of him.

A chill runs down my spine. I shiver. Words bubble up in my throat. 'Why are you always so harsh with me?'

'I'm not being harsh with you, Lana. For you, I'd die a thousand times. You'll never know how lonely I was without you, but you have to understand that I am only strong when I am certain you are safe. And you are only safe when you are innocent. You can never come to me. Always I will make the journey to you. The knowledge you are looking for is poison. It will seep into your very essence. Just this once allow me to act with beauty and courage, for you and Sorab.'

He is a broken soul. I walk up to him, and immediately he sweeps me into his arms and presses me against the hard expanse of his chest. I breathe in the scent of him, and feel again that passionate desire to be one with him. When our bodies are so fused together that our souls touch. I need to feel complete again. I have been for so many days unwhole.

'Oh, Blake.'

He lifts me into his arms, I wrap mine around his neck, and he walks me to our bed. 'Your fingers are freezing,' he says.

'Sorry.'

'Don't be.'

God, hot tears are trickling down my cheeks.

He bends his head, his shadows spilling over me. I hear the blood pounding in his temples, and he kisses my tears. 'Dew drops,' he whispers. 'I never thought it could ever be like this.'

I swallow and try to stop the tears but they won't halt.

He lays me on the bed. 'It always surprises me how silky your hair is,' he says softly to himself.

This has to be enough to pull us through. This must.

'It feels like a dream. As if you are unreal. I couldn't bear it if I woke up and you were gone,' he murmurs.

'It's not a dream. Do you believe that two people can share a love that is so deep that nothing can ever take it away?'

He doesn't answer me. Instead he looks into my eyes with so much love my heart quivers. The look changes. My tears stop, the blood begins to pound in my head.

'No need for words, Lana.'

He is right. There never was a need. His finger lightly strokes my throat. I draw breath sharply. I have been starving for his touch. He lets his finger rest on the desperate pulse. The tenderness in the gesture captivates me and starts the red-hot ache between my thighs. His mouth moves in closer and closer until his lips meet mine. I open my mouth to taste him. Ah...

He enters my soul.

In the shadows of our bedroom, time stills.

Four

I wake up in total darkness, shivering and realize instantly that I am blindfolded and naked. My hands are tied behind my back, but my legs are free. My nostrils are full of the smell of damp soil and dead leaves. Rocks and branches are digging into my back. It is eerily silent. I have no memory of how I got here. Where is Blake? Where is Sorab?

Suddenly, the air is pierced by a wail, despairing, monotone, and distant.

What the hell is that?

I freeze, bewildered and petrified. Precious seconds pass, with me holding my breath, staring into the blackness of the blindfold. Then: the knowledge, something's coming. An abomination—stalking, circling.

My lips move. 'Oh God!'

It is coming for me. It is almost upon me. The terror is indescribable. Frantically, I rub my face against the ground, gouging my cheeks on sharp stones. The blindfold shifts fractionally, but enough for me to make out that I am in a dark forest.

I scramble to my feet, swaying, my hands tied behind my back, and lurch away into the spooky shadows. The cold wind whips my face. Branches and leaves slap my bare body. I slip on moss, sprawl on the ground, pick myself up, and run blindly. In a panic, I glance backward, but it is impossible to see anything. The blackness is so thick. But I know it is still coming. I feel it in the chill that goes out like long tentacles before it to envelop me.

I take great gasping breaths: my lungs are on fire. Suddenly I hear men's voices chanting, low and guttural, and I immediately start running towards the sound. They are gathered around a large bonfire in a clearing not far away. All of them are in long black and red robes with hoods, which are pulled so low down over their faces, it is impossible to see them. There is an air of menace about them. I remember them. I have seen them at that party. They all know more than they will tell.

They are the brotherhood of El.

Far away in the distance I see a lantern. I should have gone towards the lantern. But it is too late. They have all turned to look at me. I stare at them, appalled, and terrified, and consumed with horror. They begin to advance. I turn around and run. I hear them behind me. They are faster than me. I hear them closing in, their heavy grunts. They are almost upon me.

I stumble and fall on the ground among roots and creepers. They surround me. I look from one faceless figure to the other with abject fear.

 26

'You cannot escape.'

I freeze. Oh God. No! That voice. I know that voice. I look into the darkness inside his hood. There is movement. Shiny black eyes moving to look at me. I recognize those eyes.

'But you are dead.'

An unpleasant wet, rasping sound comes from him. The rest of the group fall on me. Hands everywhere, on my breasts, between my legs. I kick and struggle, but it is no use. The clawing and yanking are impossible to resist. They make a whispering sound. Insidious and unspeakably horrible.

They are taking me down, down into the freezing pits of hell.

Suddenly I hear a cry. A baby. My baby. My Sorab.

The hands still, and they turn towards the voice. It is not me they want... It was never me.

I see Blake standing there with Sorab.

No, no, no. Quick, quick, do something. Run. I open my mouth and scream to warn him but no sound comes. They have taken my voice. It's too late. I'm too late. I begin to howl silently.

I feel hands on me. 'Wake up. It's just a dream.'

My eyes snap open and Blake is peering down at me. I stare at him in confused terror, my head full of gravel and evil. Then I throw my arms around him and clutch at him desperately.

He tries to lay me back on the pillows, but I can't let go of him. I pull back just enough to look at him. 'I am afraid for you.'

'There is nothing to be afraid of.' His voice is tender. He cradles me in his arms and gently sweeps away the hair sticking to my damp forehead and cheeks. 'It's over. It's over,' he croons.

But I am full of terror. The dream had been so real. 'The men. The hooded men... In the woods. Who are they?'

He frowns. 'What men?'

'They want you back.'

'It was just a nightmare, Lana. There are no hooded men. You're safe. There is—'

'Your father. He was alive.'

A bleak look comes into his eyes. 'My father is dead.' His voice is flat and lifeless.

I rest my forehead against his chest and begin to cry.

Again and again he reassures me, 'It was just a dream. Just a nightmare,' until I fall asleep clasped in his arms.

When I wake up again it is with a premonition that something is wrong. Raw fear. I glance at the bedside clock. It is the early hours of the morning. A warning burns in my head. I don't dismiss it. I scramble out of bed, pull on Blake's discarded shirt and run into Sorab's room. It is still early and the child is fast asleep. Softly, I open the door and hurry down the corridor. Blake is in the dining room working, bent over a piece of paper. He lifts his head, sees me, and gets to his feet suddenly.

'What's wrong?'

'Nothing,' I say, but I run towards him and throw my arms around his waist. It is true nothing is wrong. So what is the little prickling at the back of my neck, as if someone was watching me, all about then? Is this the calm before the storm? I feel my stomach in knots.

'Don't become a slave to your fears, Lana,' he whispers into my hair.

As if by magic I feel the fear slinking away. Everything is all right. Blake is fine, Sorab is fine and I am fine. Nothing is wrong. It must be just my own overwrought senses. I know it is because I don't have all the facts. There is so much I don't know.

I look up into his face. 'Shall I make you something to eat?'

'No. The only thing I am hungry for is you,' he says, taking the lobe of my ear between his teeth. 'I simply can't seem to get enough of you. I want to devour you all the fucking time.'

It is tempting. Just let him fill me up. Make me forget. So we end up in bed and for a while I do forget, but afterwards I find myself exactly where I started. With a whole pile of unanswered questions.

'I'd like us to finish that conversation we started the other day.'

'Maybe another time, Lana,' he says quietly.

We lie facing the ceiling in silence and the longer the silence stretches the more lost and alone I start to feel. I think of what we have just done—it is so vivid in my mind—and yet we could

be strangers now. I have to stop myself from rolling away from him, curling up into a ball, and just crying my eyes out. I simply want to help. I am his woman. Not his toy.

Why the silent treatment? I haven't done anything wrong. As the seconds tick by I start to fume silently. If I was Victoria he would tell me. I would enter the forbidden realms with him. I become jealous and sad all at once. But more angry than sad. I sit up and glance down furiously at him.

He turns to look at me. Questioning. Slightly puzzled. His thoughts obviously elsewhere.

I swivel my eyes away from him.

He reacts by catching my hand and pulling me down to his chest. 'What's wrong?'

There is no avoiding him while he is so in my face, and anyway I don't want to avoid him. I want a confrontation. Molded into his chest I crane my neck away from him and glare into his stare.

'You know,' I bite out fiercely, and try to twist away, but he brings his other arm around and, effortlessly, I am a total prisoner.

'If you carry on I'm going to have to fuck you again.'

'That's your answer to everything, isn't it? Out of bed I am of no use to you, am I?'

His expression changes. 'What the fuck are you talking about?'

'I don't understand you. You say you love me and you can't imagine your life without me, but you won't tell me anything. I'm sick of being locked

out, Blake. Honestly, it's tearing me up inside. Do you think I am too dumb to understand? Is that it?'

'No, it's not that—' he interjects.

But I am not done. 'In your heart of hearts you think I'm not good enough, one of the unwashed masses. How stupid of me to ever think that we could be equal partners in a relationship. I'm just a doll to you, aren't I? One day you'll get bored of playing with me, and then you'll just put me away and totally forget I even exist.'

Hot tears begin to gather in my eyes. I try to blink them away. I am not going to cry, but the more I try to stop the more sorry I feel for myself and the faster they spill out.

He does a surprising thing. It stops my blubbering instantly. He fists my hair and lures my head lower until it is inches away from his face, and then he lifts his head, and licks my tears. First one cheek, then the other.

My reaction is instant and unexpected: fresh desire sizzles through me.

'Don't... Don't ever again say such things. They were true once, but not anymore. In fact, I don't believe they were ever true. From that first night I saw you, I had a reaction to you that I have never had with anyone else. You took my breath away.

'I tried to tell myself that it was because you were so extraordinarily beautiful, but I've been with so many beautiful women, some who have brazenly thrown themselves at my feet, others who have played hard to get, and then there were

31

the truly shy ones, but never have I felt that irresistible need to brand them as mine.

'To lock them away and never let another man near them, let alone touch them. When I met you the rest of the world stopped existing. There was only you and I in my world. I wanted nothing else.'

He presses his forehead against mine, his words curling softly around us. I feel him everywhere. I love him so much it feels as if I should scream it from the rooftops. And yet I worry—my life has taught me that every time I love something, even if it be an animal, my heart will eventually be wrung out and broken.

'You must believe that I am telling you the truth. My heart was in a coffin, safe, dark, motionless...until I found you in a secret place, among the shadows of my soul. You saved me.'

He smiles softly and weaves his fingers through mine, his brows dipped low. I stare into his sad eyes. He has laid his heart at my feet. How would I have thought that he would turn out to be a gentle warrior? Love doesn't keep a record of wrongs. My heart melts. I forgive him.

'So why do you hide so much away from me, then?'

He sighs softly. 'If you knew a room was full of needles, would you let Sorab crawl in it?'

I frown. 'I'm not a baby.'

'Let me make myself clearer. I am afraid for you. I am afraid you will be taken away from me. Even the thought of losing you makes me feel sick to my stomach. You are the only person I can ever

imagine myself with now. If all else—the mansions, the mines, the cars, the business, the yachts, the planes—perished and you remained, I could still continue, but if everything else remained, but you were gone, I'd be a broken man.'

His eyes are suddenly wet. He has never cried before. It breaks my heart. He is my love, my heart, my everything. I will leave it for now. I must know, but I will find out on my own. Somehow I will find out.

'Could you not sleep last night?'

'No, there is too much to do. The phones never stop ringing. People from all over the world offering condolences.' His lips twist bitterly. 'If only they knew.'

'When is the funeral?'

'Day after tomorrow.'

'Where?'

'New York.'

'When do we leave?'

'You're not coming.' His voice is suddenly hard.

I step away from him. 'Why not?'

'Because you never take your beloved gerbil to a viper's den.'

'But I want to be with you.'

'I'm only going for a day. I'll be back the next day.'

I gaze up at him. 'Blake, I want to be with you during that time.'

'No.'

I cross my arms. 'So you don't want me at the funeral?'

'No, I don't.'

'All right, I will come with you but I won't go to the funeral.'

He shakes his head. 'No. Then I'll be worrying about you in New York.'

'All right. I won't leave the hotel.'

'You'll be bored.'

'I'll read and I'll order room service.'

That takes the wind right out of his sails. 'Why do you want to come so bad?'

'Because I want to be with you during that time. I think it is important.'

'All right. But you have to promise that you won't leave the hotel without me.'

'I promise.'

'What about Sorab?'

'If it is only for one night I'll leave him with Billie.'

He frowns.

'Blake, if you don't take me with you I will fly there on my own.'

Suddenly he looks tired. 'I can never resist you. Yeah, you can come.'

'Thank you.'

'Don't make me regret it.'

'By doing what?'

'By leaving the hotel or making me worry about you.' He looks at me warningly.

'I won't. When are we leaving?'

'Tomorrow.'

 34

Five

At first, I am amazed by the suite. Wow! This is what forty-five thousand dollars a night buys! So: top of the list are 360-degree views of Manhattan through bulletproof, floor-to-ceiling windows. I walk through the tall, spacious rooms alone, in a daze. The attention to detail is mind-boggling. The master bedroom is made from hundreds of thousands of painstakingly cut and ironed straws! Yes, very beautiful, but God!

Another room has calfskin leather walls. All the walls of the library are covered in French lacquer. The bathroom has an infinity bath and each sink is cut from one solid crystal piece. I lie on the horsehair mattress. Very, very comfortable. I open the lid of the grand piano and let my fingers trail tunelessly on the gleaming keys. I stand for ages on the balcony seven hundred feet high up looking down on the entire sprawling, throbbing city below my feet. I look at the book I have brought along and pass it by. And wonder what Blake is up to.

Eventually I get so lonely and bored I Skype Billie.

'How's Sorab?'

'Asleep. The shot of vodka did the trick.'

'I don't know that that's even funny, Bill.'

Billie laughs. 'He has to start sometime.'

'Yeah, when he's thirty.'

'So how's it going?'

'Well, Blake is busy meeting people, arranging stuff, and I am here bored out of my mind at the hotel.'

'You don't have the baby hanging around your neck—why don't you go sight-seeing?'

I sigh. 'I kind of promised I wouldn't leave the hotel.'

'What?' she splutters. 'Are you kidding me? You are in the Big Apple and you're not going out?'

'Forget it, Bill. I've promised. He didn't even want to bring me until I promised. We'll come another time. It's a bad time with the funeral and everything.'

'It's hardly a promise.'

'Don't start, please.'

'Why don't you at least go use the sauna or the pool, hmm?'

'Might do. I'm a bit hungry. Maybe I will go down and get something to eat at the restaurant. But first, do you want a tour of the suite? It's amazing.'

'Go on then.'

I end the call after the tour and go down to the lobby. I am standing at the plate glass window looking out when a man comes to stand beside me.

'You look like a child outside a cake shop,' says a strongly accented, man's voice.

I turn my head to look at him. He is tall, lantern-jawed and wearing jeans and a cowboy hat. He might be from down South.

'Texas,' he says.

'I see.'

'British?'

I smile. 'Yes, it is that obvious, huh?'

'I'm just about to fly to London on business.'

'Oh really?'

'Do you know what they say here about the difference between British accents and the hillbilly accent? When you hear a British accent add fifty to the IQ and when you hear a hillbilly accent subtract fifty.'

I laugh.

'Carlton Starr. Welcome to America.'

'Lana Bloom. Thank you.'

'Will you keep me company while I take some tea?'

'Ah... I'm actually with someone.'

He throws his head back and roars with genuine laughter. 'Of course you are. It never crossed my mind that a woman as beautiful as you would be without someone. Come on, I'll tell you all about my country if you'll tell me all about yours.'

I smile. From the corners of my eyes I can see Brian seated in one of the plush chairs. He appears to be reading a book. I know I am totally safe and I am not leaving the hotel premises.

'OK,' I agree.

Immediately, he puts a guiding hand just under my elbow. That does make me feel as if he is being a little too familiar, but Billie did say that Americans were super friendly. They can become your best friend on the first encounter, was her verdict.

I have taken no more than a few steps in the direction he is guiding me towards when I freeze. My stop is so sudden that Carlton's body nudges into me making me stumble slightly, forcing him, in turn, to grab me by the waist. All this while my eyes are caught by Blake's. He is staring at me with a look I have never seen.

Carlton whispers in my ear. 'I guess that's your someone.'

Blake strides towards me, his face as hostile and unyielding as gray granite. When he reaches us, he glances at Carlton with crushing clear-eyed contempt before snatching my wrist, and dragging me away. Blake moves at such speed across the foyer that I am forced to gallop to keep up. I am so embarrassed my entire face flames up. I feel like a child who is on her way to be punished.

At the lift he hits the call button and waits. A staff member comes to stand beside us. He lets his eyes slide off Blake and rest on me a while before lowering them to hide his expression. My dignity is in tatters and I am certain everyone is looking at me. Blake enters the lift with me in tow.

'Would you mind waiting for the next one?' Blake says coldly, when the man tries to enter behind us.

The man nods and hurriedly steps backwards. The doors close. I pull my hand out of Blake's grasp and rubbing my wrists ask, 'What the hell was that all about?'

He lets his eyes swing down in my direction. His voice is a tightly controlled don't fuck with me. 'Shouldn't I be asking you that?'

'What exactly are you suggesting?'

The doors open and, taking my wrist in his hand again, he drags me into our suite. I whirl around to face him.

'What's the matter with you, Blake?'

'What the fuck do you think is the matter with me?' he roars. 'I leave you for a few hours and you start picking stray men up in the hotel lobby?'

'Are you mad? Picking stray men up? It wasn't like that. I *told* him I was with someone. He just wanted to have some company while he was having tea.'

'You're not a child so you must be stupid.'

My jaw drops. 'You're crazy. It's not like I went up to his room.'

His eyes glitter dangerously and his jaw hardens even further.

'For God's sake, Blake, Brian was there. We were just going to have some tea. He wanted me to tell him about Britain. He's going to do business there. That's all.'

'You let him touch you.'

'On my elbow!'

He comes towards me. 'How can I put this politely? If I catch you trying to have tea with strange men or letting them put their hands on your elbow or any other part of your body again I will put you over my knees and tan your backside.'

I gasp. The unfairness of it is unbelievable. 'So I can never again have tea with any other man even under the most innocent context?'

He crosses his arms. 'Exactly.'

I begin to laugh. 'This is madness. No, I don't accept. Don't try to make out I was doing something wrong. He was just a nice guy.'

'Ah, why didn't you tell me? A nice guy? In that case, go ahead. Go down now and have tea with him. I'll call down to the pretty receptionist and have her come up for some tea with me.'

A fire roars into my belly. Fucking bastard. He wants other women. The cheek of it. I stare at him open-mouthed with shock while he simply looks at me with a smug expression. I exhale the breath I am holding. Fuck him.

'All right, I will,' I snarl, and stride towards the door. A hand shoots out and catches my wrist. I am slammed into his body. His face is inches away from mine and his eyes are dangerously stormy. We glare at each other.

'Are you trying to drive me crazy?' he growls.

'No.'

'I don't want any man near you, let alone to touch you. God, I can't even bear it when I see them looking at you. You're mine.'

'He wasn't trying to bed me.'

He closes his eyes in exasperation. 'You don't understand men. Whenever one approaches you he has already thought of bedding you.'

'So you think the receptionist is pretty.'

'Maybe.'

'What?' I gasp.

He laughs. 'I was teasing you. There is no one else but you, Lana. You've got me so I can't even think straight.' His eyes move hungrily over my face. 'I crave your mouth, your skin, your hair. Every morning I wake up ravenous for you, then I pace around during the day starving for you, and at night just after I've had you I start to crave your hot, sweet body all over again. Do you really believe any other woman could nourish me? The last thing on my mind is having sex with another woman.'

Inside I melt. 'But you think she is pretty?'

'Not really. Sorab is better looking.'

'But you must have noticed her to mention it.'

He groans. 'Oh for fuck's sake, Lana, I just said the first thing that came into my mind.'

'I just want you to know that I don't appreciate being dragged through hotel lobbies like some recalcitrant child.'

He runs his knuckle tenderly down my cheek. 'Then don't flirt with strange men in silly hats.'

'For the last time, I wasn't flirting.'

In response he cups my buttocks.

'I've really missed you today,' I say a little breathlessly.

'I bet you say that to all the boys,' he says, as his mouth moves down to crush mine with such passion that my feet lift off the ground.

Six

I am given a choice between the four-starred Le Bernadin with its formal dress code and its prestigious three Michelin stars or a red sauce joint in Greenwich Village called Carbone, where, Blake tells me, excess is de rigueur and the diner must abandon any hope of moderation. After staying inside the hotel all day, of course, I choose Carbone. They book thirty days out, but, of course, Laura, who seems forever on the job, swings us a table.

'Doesn't that girl ever sleep?' I ask.

'I never thought to ask,' Blake says, shrugging into his jacket.

I look at him standing there in a charcoal suit and a black, turtle neck sweater and—gorgeousness overload—my stomach does a little flip-flop.

Carbone is packed, lively and loud. Designed to look like the stage set of an old-fashioned Mafia movie, it carries that instinct for entertainment throughout. From the floor pattern to their choice of music—songs my grandmother used to listen

to: Sinatra, the rat pack—and strutting, jovial waiters dressed in shiny Liberace style maroon tuxedos. They show us to our table in the VIP section: a rear room made to look like the kind of place where powerful Godfathers might have met—red and black tiled floors, brick walls and no windows.

Deeply fragrant shellfish reduction stock wafts up from the next table as we sit. My eyes are drawn to four flushed men tucking into their food. On other tables the waiters seem to be character actors who have perfected the art of the flashy, bossy restaurant captain. I watch them, with cocky smarminess, lean in conspiratorially, improvise dialog, and kiss the tips of their fingers, as they make wildly exaggerated promises of excellence to sell their wares and smile approvingly when their recommendations are taken.

We are handed menus that are at least three feet long.

Blake orders the veal parm and I am ruthlessly cajoled into having the lobster fra diavolo (the best you'll taste in your lifetime). A four hundred dollar bottle of Barollo is opened with flourish, the cork sniffed appreciatively, and offered to Blake to try. He arches his eyebrow at me. My glass is filled. We clink glasses.

'To us,' Blake says.

'To us,' I echo. The wine is big and rich and very strong.

'What was your day like then?' I ask.

'Grim. I spent all day with people I'd rather not ever see, and then I come back to the hotel and catch you flirting with some hick in a cowboy hat.'

'I wasn't flirting.'

His eyebrows shoot up. 'So, what did you do, besides flirting with strange men?'

'I wasn't flirting!' I say forcefully.

He smiles. 'I love it when you are fierce.'

'Well, I don't like it when you are. You are downright scary.'

'Then don't piss me off.'

I sigh. 'I went downstairs because I couldn't read. I was worried about you.'

A waiter comes with appropriate cutlery for us.

'I wouldn't like you to get bored while I am at work. Is there anything you'd like to do with your time?'

'I want to set up a charity to help children,' I say, quite timidly.

'Really? What sort of charity?'

I lean forward eagerly. 'I haven't decided yet, but I do know that I want to make a huge difference.' I take a sip of wine. 'If you were me, what would you do? What is the most significant thing I can do for the children of the world?'

'If it is the children of the poorest countries, then I'd give them the most precious commodity in the world—water,' he suggests quietly.

'Water?'

'Yes, clean fresh water from tap spigots. Currently two million children die every year from

drinking unsafe water, but those figures are about to go through the roof.'

'Why?'

'There is a global water crisis and water is being privatized.'

That surprises me. I know so little. I had much to learn before I could set up my charity. We are still deep in discussion about the mechanics of starting a trust fund when the food arrives. I lean back and finally understand what Billie meant when she said the food portions in American restaurants are the size of garden sheds.

Blake's veal is shock-and-awe huge and served with a fried shaft of bone, ovals of browned buffalo mozzarella, and bright red, fresh tomato sauce. Mine is a two and a half pound lobster that has been de-shelled, cooked with Calabrian chilies and Cognac, and piled back into the shell. It is polished and glistening and reeking of garlic butter. Bread like Mama used to make arrives.

Blake and I tuck into the delicious food. It *is* the best lobster I have tasted.

For dessert we order zabaglione. It is prepared using the yolks from goose eggs in a round-bottomed copper pot over a flame at the table. Afterwards, I have homemade limoncello and Blake knocks back a fig grappa. By the time we leave the premises I am feeling decidedly tipsy.

'Can't wait to get you into bed,' I mumble into his neck.

He looks down at me indulgently and chuckles. 'I'm so glad you're such a greedy little thing.'

We get back to the hotel and fall into each other's arms.

'You are my dream,' he whispers in my ear. 'You have made me who I am.' Neither of us mentions the father he dispatched into the next world for me, or the funeral that must be attended tomorrow, but it is there, silently watching, its long shadow falling over our entwined bodies.

Stay if you must, but I will never pretend I am not glad a predator like you is gone from this world. And that because you are gone, my son is safe.

That night I wake up to sudden movement beside me. I sit up and in the light from the moon I can make out that Blake is caught in a nightmare and thrashing about in distress.

'I killed him!' he yells.

I shake him awake urgently. His bleary eyes focus on my face, and for a micro-second he looks at me with fear and horror, and then his brain gets into gear, and he recognizes me. With a look of relief he clasps me to his body with such force that my lungs can't expand to take the next breath.

'Hey.'

He loosens his hold. 'Oh, Lana, Lana, Lana,' he sighs.

'Were you dreaming about your father?'

'No.'

A cold hand comes to clutch my heart. No. I close my eyes with anguish. I cannot not love him.

But oh God! Oh God! Has he killed someone else? Who is this man that I love?

'Who then?' I ask fearfully.

'I don't know him. He is covered in blood.'

My body sags with relief. It was just a nightmare. How incredibly frightened I had been as I formed those two words, 'Who then'. Tears of relief start running down my face. He feels them against his skin and pulls me away from his body.

He touches them with wonder. 'Why?'

I don't tell him the truth. Because for a moment I thought I was in love with a monster.

'Because I love you,' I say. But that, too, is the truth. I loved him even in that corrosive, soul-destroying moment when I thought he was a monster.

Seven

It is Brian who gives me the exact time the funeral will be shown on TV. I tune the TV to the appropriate channel and settle myself in front of the large flat-screen to wait. The film clip is remarkable for two reasons: its brevity and the fact that it is filmed in church. A suitably sober woman's voice announces that the funeral of an industry leader was held that afternoon.

The camera rests for a moment on the widow and I see Blake's mother properly for the first time. In those few seconds it is obvious to me that Blake is her favorite son. Wearing a matt black coat she stands very close to him and seems almost to lean on him. He appears very tall, broad, and unapproachable. Almost I don't recognize that stern, imposing man!

A little farther away Marcus stands beside his immaculate and totally expressionless wife. They are flanked by their two children. I look for Quinn and I think I recognize him. The family resemblance is strong. He is the one standing a little to the left of Blake. Blake seems very protective of him. Then there is a quick shot of the casket and the news item is over and the Barringtons slip seamlessly into their manufactured obscurity. The entire news clip is another carefully crafted PR exercise from a notoriously secretive family.

I switch off the TV and time seems to stop as I wait for him to return.

I try to read, but cannot arouse any interest in the words before me. I put on some music and try to relax in the bath. But I am too wound up and after a few minutes I get out and dress in a blue blouse and black skirt. I hear him at the door and run out to greet him.

He takes off his long dark coat and stands in his funereal garments. His face is grim. I want to run to him and bury my face in his neck, but he seems unreachable. I stare at him without comprehension. He bewilders me, infuriates, makes me feel weak and vulnerable, and yet he is my hero and the strength that carries me through the day.

'How was it?' I ask instead.

'As expected.' His lips curl into an expression I have not seen before.

'Everything went well, then?'

He nods. 'Let's get drunk together,' he says.

I look into his eyes. He looks furious about something. 'OK.'

He goes to the phone and orders up a bottle of Scotch.

They must have asked which brand.

 50

'Just bring your best,' he says impatiently, and puts the phone back on the hook. I go to hold him and he puts his hand out as if to ward me off. 'Don't touch me,' he says, and I freeze.

He runs his hand through his hair. 'I just need a shower. Meet me in the bedroom,' he says, and turning away goes to the bathroom.

The bottle arrives with two glasses and a bucket of ice while he is in the shower. I tip the man, and taking everything into the bedroom, pour two generous measures into the glasses. I can hear the sound of the shower. At any other time I would have gone into the shower and joined him, but I can see that today he is different. He seems like forbidden territory. I shudder. Something has happened that has affected him deeply. I pace the bedroom. Look at myself in the mirror. I look OK.

He comes out and leans in the doorway in a towel loosely hitched around his lean hips. Wow! Divine. I love this man with wet hair. The blood starts to pound in my eardrums. When will the half-naked sight of him cease to affect me this way?

'You are still dressed,' he notes with raised eyebrows.

I say nothing—simply, slowly, start undressing. First the blouse goes over my head, then the skirt ends up at my feet, the bra gets flung away, and finally the knickers go the way of everything else. The balcony windows are open and the slight breeze scatters goose pimples on my skin. I look at him as he approaches me. God! He's so fucking delectable. I watch the muscles rippling as he loses the towel. He stops inches away and twirls my hair in his fingers. The nearness of him makes me want to lick that pulse beating at the base of his throat. That is the only real conversation we have. That pulse that never lies to me. When it beats, I know he wants me, bad.

'Want ice cubes in your drink?' I ask, huskily.

He smiles and shakes his head. 'The ice cubes are for you.'

I smile back. 'Really?'

'Really,' he drawls, and pulls me towards him until I feel his entire length and his hot, hard shaft presses into my abdomen. His mouth descends. My hands rise up and entwine around his neck and we kiss. We kiss. And we kiss. Both he and I know. This is the magic staircase by which he can climb back from whatever dark place he has been in.

He lifts me off the ground and lays me on the bed. I grab his thighs. He looks at me, surprised. I lift myself off the bed and take his beautiful cock in my mouth. He inhales sharply. I straighten my head so he can have a full view of my lips curled tightly around his thick meat. When I look up I meet his eyes. The intensity of his gaze hits me in the bones. I suck so hard my cheeks hollow in, and experience heady power when I see him surrender to pleasure, to me. I swirl my tongue around his shaft confidently.

'Open your legs,' he growls.

Obediently, I spread my legs and show him what he wants to see, but I do not stop sucking and

pulling hard at his meat. He eyes my open sex avidly. His face contorts. His body buckles, and he spurts inside my mouth. Even when his eyes have turned languorous, I don't take my mouth away. I hold the semi-hard cock in my mouth and I gaze up at him. He gathers himself, touches my face tenderly, and pulls out of my mouth.

Deliberately, I lick my lips.

He grins wickedly, and turns away. My eyes follow him as he prowls around, buck naked, over to the bottle of whiskey. Tipping it over the ice bucket he starts pouring it out. I rise up on my elbow.

'What're you doing?'

He looks at me over his raised arm. 'Fixing myself a drink,' he says, and continues wasting the whiskey until there is less than a quarter of the bottle left. He drops half a fistful of ice cubes into my glass and brings the bottle and the glass into the bed. He walks towards my body on his knees and holds out my glass. I take a sip—the alcohol is strong, but goes down smooth. I watch him swig straight from the bottle, his head thrown back, his throat strong and powerfully masculine, his skin glowing like polished bronze. What a sight he is. His manhood erect, his thighs rippling and powerful, his shoulders broad.

Always in moments like this he reminds of a Greek god.

He swings the bottle down to hip level, wipes his mouth with the back of his hand, and catches my eyes. His are hooded, dark and full of desire.

There is something in him that is different. He looks into my eyes. I feel myself burn under his gaze. A fluttering in my belly. I am nervous. Why? But I am also turned on. Unbelievably excited by this new him.

'Now what?'

He breaks eye contact and looks at the bottle. Very deliberately, he removes the metal ring broken off from the bottle cap and puts it on the bedside table.

He lies on his elbow beside me. The bottle touches my cheek. It is cold. I turn and look into his eyes. What is in them thrills me.

'Do you know that far, far more erotic than a cock inside you is to have an ordinary household object put into you? My excited, scandalized eyes swivel to the bottle and back to him. What I see in his eyes electrifies me.

'Yeah?'

He smiles slowly. 'Yeah.'

I nod and he swipes the pad of his thumb along my bottom lip. Suddenly he is on my mouth, rough, rough... The bottle goes away from my cheek. I part my thighs and gasp into his mouth when he inserts it into me. Fuck me! Cold and hard and erotic. Very, very erotic. I gape at him.

He lifts his head and watches me as he puts his hand under my buttocks and lifts me off the bed so I feel the liquid gurgling into me. I want to cover my mouth. 'Oh!'

'Yes, "Oh",' he murmurs, but his breathing is ragged, his eyes liquid.

When the bottle is empty he tosses it away.

'What does it feel like?'

'It's sexy.'

He laughs. 'All illicit trespasses are,' he says.

Gloriously naked, he reaches for a handful of ice cubes. He runs them over the heated flesh of my sex and inserts them one by one into me, while I squirm helplessly. Then he kneels between my legs and begins to drink from my pussy. The process is a slow sensual assault. Lick, lick, suck, lick, lick, suck, suck as the cold liquid dribbles out of me. I arch my back.

'Yes, right there... Yes.'

The sensations are so foreign, the numbing effect of the cubes, his searing tongue, sometimes teeth, the sloshing of the alcohol. I am so caught up in the intense sensations I hardly recognize the high-pitched animal sounds coming out of my mouth.

'We're going to take it one level higher.' He lays down beside me. 'Clench your muscles and come sit on my mouth.'

Very carefully I sit up and clenching hard I move over to his face and position myself over his mouth. Having to clench my muscles while he is slowly drinking the dribble is strangely unnerving, and filthy, but exquisite. As if there are no barriers between us. He wants everything I've got. Even my juices. Suddenly he swoops upwards and catching my sex in a hard suction pulls me down on top of him. He grinds my sex over his mouth.

I tense so all the liquid does not gush out, but it is impossible to keep control of my body—it starts contracting and spiraling out of control. I come in a gush. I look down and he is greedily gobbling all the liquids that are pouring out of me. I lift my sex away from his mouth and look at him: smeared with alcohol and all my juices. Then he pulls me back down and licks me clean.

'My Lana,' he says, his eyes glowing possessively.

Eight

I return to England inspired by Carbone and decide to cook a feast of senses for Blake. He is given strict instructions to come home early. Two hours ago I fried some rabbit, pancetta, onions, garlic, sage in a pan and tipped a bottle of Sangiovese into it. Once the mixture was simmering I added rosemary, thyme, some sticks of cinnamon, and cloves.

Now the hare has started to collapse into the sauce, which has become as sticky as runny honey and will nicely coat the handmade rigatoni that Francesca brought in today. I plan to serve this rich, pungent dish with a whole artichoke, slathered in warm olive oil and lemon juice and sprinkled with chopped mint.

In the oven I have a fresh peach tart to be served with Italian gelato.

I glance over at Sorab. He is rubbing his eyes. We were down in the park all afternoon and he looks as if he could do with a nap, but I don't allow him to sleep. This way he will sleep the night through. I hear Blake at the door.

'Daddy's home,' I announce rapturously, and, scooping Sorab off the floor, I run out to the front door to meet him.

'Hey,' he says, pulling a large smile into his face.

Sorab begins to wriggle and lifts his arms in his father's direction. Blake takes him from me and lifting him high into the air blows raspberries on his belly, while Sorab laughs, squirms, and kicks.

He turns his head to look at me and sniffs the air. 'What's that?'

'That,' I grin, 'is your dinner.'

'It smells amazing.'

Holding Sorab to the side of his body he bends and kisses me, bathing my body in a languorous, sensuous glow. There is delicious food waiting in the kitchen, my man is home, my son is in his arms: there is nothing more in this world I could possibly ask for.

Blake reaches for my hand and suddenly stills, his eyes narrowing. 'What's this?' he asks softly, touching the plaster on my finger.

'It's nothing. I nicked my finger while I was cutting some vegetables.'

He frowns and envelops my hand in his. 'I don't want you cooking anymore. I'll get Laura to sort a chef out for you tomorrow.'

'No,' I say immediately. 'I don't want a chef. I enjoyed cooking for us today. I don't want a nanny either. I just want it to be the three of us.'

He looks at me, his jaw is tight.

'Just for a while, Blake. Please.'

'OK. For a while. We are moving to One Hyde Park Place next week anyway.'

'What?'

'It's much better there. You will have access to the Mandarin Oriental's chef.'

'Can't we just stay here for a little while longer? Everything has happened so fast and I'm still so confused about so much. This is like my home now. I feel comfortable here, and Billie's just around the corner.'

He puts an arm around my waist. 'If it makes you happy to stay here then we will stay here for a while longer. But we will have to move eventually.'

'Thank you.' I smile up at him. 'I've got a surprise for you.'

'Yeah?'

I give him the box. 'Give me that child.'

He hands over Sorab to me, opens the box, and looks up at me quizzically. 'Slippers?'

'Yeah. It's comfy. For around the home.'

'Like a grandfather?'

I laugh happily. 'You couldn't look like a grandfather if you tried. Now try them on.' Sorab takes the box and bites the corner while he takes off his shoes and puts on the slippers.

'Well?'

'Like walking on air.'

'Excellent.'

He gazes into my eyes—his are dark and moist. 'Do you know I have never worn slippers?

'Never?'

'Never. You've totally changed my life, Lana.'

'I'm not finished,' I say and pass him the next package.

He opens it. 'Sweats?'

'Hmmnnnn...'

I stand and watch him strip off his office wear and get into the dark blue sweats.

'What do you think?'

'Edible,' I say, and I really mean it. Low-slung pants on slim sexy hips. A little bit of skin shows and I reach out and touch it.

Instantly, he looks deep into my eyes, his expression changing.

'I've got other plans for you tonight,' I tell him and retract my hand. 'Here,' I say and hand the baby over to him.

He takes Sorab and goes off to the living room. I return to the kitchen. Food will be ready in twenty minutes. By the time I put the stretched bread lightly brushed with tomato sauce into the oven, Sorab is sound asleep on his father's body. While Blake puts him down for the night, I turn down the lights in the dining room, and stand back to admire the glow of the candles on the white table linen heavy with all kinds of foods.

Tart giardiniera in oil, olives, cured meats from the deli, salads, ribbons of fried dough dusted with powdered sugar and an intricate terrine of fruits layered with alcohol-soaked sponge. And of course, a very special bottle of red that I have opened and allowed to breathe.

The first piece I slip into his mouth. The expression of rapture and astonishment is gratifying.

'It is how I imagine the food in the paintings of Caravaggio to be—real, hearty, Roman—a bird roasted in a wood oven,' he says.

'Really?' At that moment I make up my mind to learn about art and music, to become, culturally, his equal. He will never have cause to be ashamed of me in front of his peers.

The rest of the meal becomes a dreamy evening that will forever echo in my heart. Everything was perfect. I watch Blake eat, as a mother watches her child eat. Protectively, proudly.

And he eats without inhibition or his usual control and care—cutting his food into dozens of pieces, which he then carefully picks at as if they are something dangerous. He eats with genuine pleasure, sucking the sauce off his fingers, reveling in every new flavor.

Finally, among the crumbs of our feast, Blake dips a lemon cookie into the dessert wine and brings it, still dripping golden drops, to my lips. I quickly swoop down and bite. The sweet raisin-like taste explodes on my taste buds, as a drop escapes from the side of my mouth. Before I can bring my napkin to my lips he leans in and licks the corner of my mouth. As if he is a wolf or some animal that uses its tongue to wash the body of its mate.

He carries on licking diligently until every last lingering trace is gone and still he licks until he

happens upon the two tiny drops on my neck. I stare at him. So close to me, still so foreign and yet, my whole life. This is the man I had not intended to love. And now I cannot imagine my life without him.

He raises his eyes to me. 'I couldn't understand the concept of eating food off a naked woman before. Now I can.' He slips his hand along the inside of my thigh. 'The grace of the human figure, the delicacy of its form is the perfect plate. I'd love to fill your body with all manner of food and slowly lick it off.' His fingers reach the apex of my thighs. I part my legs willingly. '*Soufflé aux fruits de la passion* on your nipples, *sabayon* sauce on your belly, caramel on your pubic bone and *bananas en papilote* between your legs.' One long finger enters me.

I blush as if he has not done far more outrageous things to me. Perhaps the thought of lying on a table and being a platter for food that will be consumed off my body is incredibly erotic. And the thought of Blake slowly licking and sucking actually makes me wet.

The finger retreats. I inhale.

He puts the finger in his mouth. I exhale.

I pour out two glasses of sambuca, place three coffee beans on their surfaces and set them alight. Over the blue flames I catch Blake's eyes. In this light they are so dark they are almost black. The intensity of his gaze makes me catch my breath. I forget about the burning drinks, until he lowers

his face without breaking eye contact and blows out the flames.

He dips his finger in the sambuca and smears it on my lips, and lifting me off the chair carries me to the bedroom to be ravished.

'The sambuca...'

'I've had enough.'

'The dishes,' I whisper into his neck.

'Tomorrow.'

'The candles...'

'Later.'

When I wake up again, it is because of a cry or a moan. I turn my head and he is not in bed. I roll out of bed and go into Sorab's room. Blake is holding him and softly crooning him back to sleep. Our eyes meet over our baby's head. His are soft, softer than I have seen them.

I wish I could capture the moment forever.

He brings one forefinger to his lips. So I don't say anything. Simply memorize that magical moment. When a man's beautiful soul is unearthed by his son. When we are all connected. He, Sorab and I.

Nine

'Tonight you get to meet my brother. We are having dinner together.'

I look at Blake, surprised. 'Quinn?'

'No, Marcus actually.' He watches me carefully.

I bite my lip. The memory of his brother's cold, blue eyes is seared into my memory forever. 'I have met him. At the hospital, when you were in a coma.'

'He told me. But briefly, right?'

'Yes, incredibly brief.'

'Didn't go too well, huh?'

'Nope. He didn't want me in the picture.'

His lips tighten. 'You *are* in the picture now. He'd better get used to it.'

'Maybe you should go on your own this time. I'm sure I'll get to meet him on other occasions.'

He puts his finger under my chin. 'You are coming tonight.'

I send Sorab over to Billie's early and I bathe and start getting ready hours before Blake is due to return. I try on a dozen outfits, but nothing looks good to my critical eye. I look at the clock. Blake

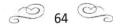

will be home soon. Black. Black always works. I hunt for something black. I find a simple black dress with a sweetheart neckline and zip myself into it.

I look at myself in the mirror unhappily. I look pale. The solution might lie with red lipstick. I apply some and blot my lips. I still don't look or feel right. There is a ball of apprehension in the pit of my stomach. It feels as if I am about to enter an exam hall unprepared. I'll stick like glue to Blake and that way I know I will be safe. My thoughts are interrupted by Blake's appearance at the bedroom door.

'Oh!' I whirl around startled. 'I didn't hear you come in.'

He grins. 'I wanted to surprise you.'

I clutch my chest dramatically. 'You succeeded. I nearly jumped out of my skin.'

He is carrying a bag that he drops on the bed on his way towards me. When he reaches me he holds me by my elbows. 'You look very, very...very...very beautiful, but that is not what you are wearing today.'

'No?'

He shakes his head slowly as his hands turn me around. For a moment I feel his finger on my bare skin, then the zip starts its downward journey. He turns me back around and gently pulls at the sleeves of the dress. It slips down my body. He winks at me.

'Love the underwear, by the way.'

'Thank you,' I reply primly.

He goes back to the bed and upends the bag he has brought with him on to the bed. A shoebox and something else drop out. The something else is soft and covered in tissue. He shakes it loose of its wrapping and my mouth parts. The dress is stunningly beautiful. Above the waist it is entirely blue appliqué lace design with a V-neck. Below the waist it is a sleek electric blue taffeta figure-hugging skirt. He holds it up.

'Fleur?'

'Of course. What'd you think?'

'Beautiful.'

He helps me get into it and touches my skin through the lace. Then he walks away and opens the shoebox. He brings it to me and, kneeling at my feet, grasps each in turn and fastens the delicate straps around my ankles. I grip his shoulders. When I am securely fastened in my new shoes he stands, and looking at me smiles with satisfaction.

He takes me to the mirror, turns me around so I can see my own reflection. Then he fastens around my throat a necklace glowing with deeply blue stones.

'Wow!'

'Sapphires,' he says. 'To match your eyes.'

I touch them wonderingly.

He reaches for a tissue and gently, as if I was made from the most fragile glass wipes off the red lipstick. My lips part to allow him access. He drops the tissue on the vanity top and picks up lip gloss. Nude. Carefully he dabs it on the insides of my lips.

When he turns me back to face the mirror, I understand what he has done. I meet his gaze with grateful eyes.

'Thank you, for selling yourself to me,' he says with a soft smile.

'Thank you for buying me.'

'I think we should live happily ever after, don't you?'

'Most definitely.'

I look at the blaze of his eyes, the belief shining in them and my heart feels as if it would burst with happiness. And for a moment I even forget the ordeal of sitting down to dinner with Marcus.

'Where are we going?' I ask nervously.

'Your favorite restaurant. The Waterside Inn.'

I smile, remembering the red carpets, the tranquil view of the river, a kindly civilized ambience, unobtrusively attentive waiters, and milk-fed lambs roasted and expertly carved into leaves of flesh at the table. 'Thank you.'

We arrive before Marcus, which is the way Blake planned it, so I would have time to settle myself. Blake parks and comes around to open my door. He helps me out and we stand a moment looking around us. The autumn wind picks up a few brown leaves swirls them in a dance drops them again a little farther down the road.

'Come on,' he says. 'I promise I won't let him eat you.'

'I'm not really scared of him.'

'That's my girl.'

The staff remember us and greet us with genuine warmth, which immediately makes me feel a little more confident. We are shown to a round corner table in the elegant waiting area. I sit back and stare unseeingly at my menu sans prix.

Soon I am accepting the complimentary glass of Michel Roux's champagne. We clink glasses.

'To tonight,' Blake says, and we sip our aperitif. It is perfectly chilled.

'Do you know what you want to eat?'

I shake my head and look again at the menu, but I cannot concentrate on the words. I will have what I had before, it was glorious—salad of crayfish tails and flaked Devon crab with melon and fresh almonds.

Butterflies flutter in my stomach. Canapés appear. I ignore them.

'The smoked eel tempura is nice,' says Blake encouragingly.

I bring it to my mouth. Chew and swallow having tasted nothing.

I shouldn't be so nervous. There is nothing he can do to me and if he disapproves of me so what?

And then Marcus appears.

Ten

Blake stands. I am not sure if I should stand, and eventually I don't. Marcus shakes his brother's hand, but also touches his shoulder in the way that politicians engaging in power games do. Then he turns and nods at me.

'Marcus, I don't believe you have been formally introduced to Lana. Lana, this is my brother, Marcus.'

'Hello,' I say. My voice comes out cold and distant.

But Marcus bends slightly from the waist, tilts his head as if it is a great honor, and allows his good-looking face to curve into a genuine open smile. He offers his hand to me. 'I have to admit I am jealous of my brother. How on earth did he pull off getting a girl as beautiful as you?'

The friendly gestures and words throw me. 'Um...' I close my mouth and take the proffered hand.

His handshake is the right shade of firm. He sits down opposite us, and starts chatting. He is utterly, utterly charming. I find myself staring at him with bewilderment. Could this be the same

man I met in the hospital? Was I in such a state of shock that I misread him? I watch him throw his head back and laugh at something Blake has said to him.

The family resemblance is very strong. They are both tall and broad, but his brother lacks the strong sense of purpose that surrounds Blake like a crackling vibrating energy. I can see now why Blake's father decided that it should be Blake who should take over the helm of leadership.

The waitress comes by. Our table is ready.

Marcus stands politely and holds his hand out to help me up. Since he is closest to the door, I have no choice but to put my hand in his. Our eyes meet. His betray nothing but a polite desire to help me up. And yet, there is tension in my body. Before I can extricate my fingers from his, I feel the tug of Blake's hand on my waist.

I look up into his eyes and I realize he was perfectly serious when he said he cannot bear any other man to touch me. Not even his brother, not even in the most innocent social setting. We are shown to our table. I slide into the long seat and Blake slides in after me.

Bread appears to my right. I point to a roll, and it is gently deposited onto my side plate. Our wine glasses are filled with straw-colored wine. Waiters start arriving with our starters. I pick up my fork. Parmesan cream with truffles. There is conversation going on around me, over me. I nod. I smile. I say thank you and I find myself drinking more than normal. Stop, right now, I tell myself.

'Have you been to the opera?' Marcus asks me. His voice is smooth.

I suddenly remember the way I was that night, and flushing bright red with embarrassment and confusion, look to Blake.

'Yes, we went to see L'incoronazione de Poppea in Venice,' Blake cuts in smoothly.

Marcus nods approvingly. 'The only place to experience Monteverdi.' He turns to me. 'Was that your first time?'

'Yes,' I mumble.

'Did you enjoy it?'

The memory makes me blush. I turn my head towards Blake, and my eyes are caught by his. There is hunger in his.

Marcus coughs delicately. I tear my eyes away. 'Yes, very much,' I say huskily.

'Freya, my wife, and I love the opera. We were at the Met for Rossini's La Cenerentola last week.'

Blake glances at me. 'Cinderella,' he says by way of explanation.

I nod gratefully.

'I'm afraid it was a grotesque, painfully anti-musical burlesque, only intermittently redeemed by virtuoso vocalism by the central waif.'

Marcus sips at his Latour.

I bite my lip. Suddenly I feel ignorant, uncultured and inferior. I realize that Blake has been careful never to let me feel less educated than he is. The truth is his world is totally different from mine. I remember Victoria telling me that no matter what I wear or do they will smell me out. In

their eyes I will never be good enough. Will I ever be able to wear this mask of apparent reticence and nonchalance that Marcus wears with such ease? Will I ever possess this studied carelessness that hides all that is real about a person? Marcus is still talking. Surreptitiously I sneak a look at Blake. He is buttering his roll and nodding. Will Blake be ashamed of me one day?

'And what about you, Lana?'

Shit. I wasn't listening. 'Um... Please excuse me. I have to go to the...loo.'

The moment I say that word, I actually feel light-headed. I remember that it was that beast, Rupert Lothian, who taught me it. His sneering words come back to me, 'This lot call it the loo.' I stand up and both men get to their feet. For a moment I look at them confused, and then I realize, of course, it is their way, an exaggerated politeness in the presence of a lady. I nod and walk towards the Ladies.

There is no one in there, and I lean against one of the walls, and close my eyes. Why am I so affected by Marcus? Why have I allowed myself to become such a mess of shattered nerves? Is it because we met in my moment of great fear and confusion that I have allowed him to grow into such a monster in my mind? I go to the basin, wash my hands and look at my own reflection.

'You have nothing to fear from him,' I tell myself. Then I take my mobile out and call Billie.

'How's it going?' she asks.

'Er... I'm not sure.'

'It's a yes or no with reptiles.'

'It's a no.'

'Hmmnnn… Your son is giving trouble.'

'What kind of trouble?'

'He doesn't want to sleep. He thinks he should be allowed to climb through the window, on to the balcony, and probably over it.'

'It's not one of his best ideas.'

'I'll say, but he is surprisingly fast for such a little thing.'

'Tie him up or something. I'll be there soon.'

'Lana. Reptiles are creatures of instinct and repetition. A mammal can out-think them any day.'

'Doesn't feel like it right now.'

'In that case give him a black eye. That always works.'

'Thanks for the advice. I'll be sure to bear it in mind.'

'You're welcome.'

'See you soon.'

'Use all your strength.'

I end the call, reapply lip gloss, and walk back to the table. Again both men stand while I seat myself. A brand new napkin has been put beside my plate. I open it and place it on my lap.

'I was just saying to Blake that both of you should come to Victoria's birthday party.'

My eyes widen. I feel the blood leaving my face.

Blake weaves his fingers through mine. I turn my head towards him.

'Victoria is Marcus's second daughter.'

I turn to face Marcus. He is looking at me innocently, but suddenly I know. He knew I would think he was referring to Blake's ex. He wanted to rattle me. But his revealing action has the opposite effect on me. I feel a little stronger. It was not knowing what I was dealing with that made me so weak. Now I know, it is better.

'When is it?'

Blake's voice is very dry. 'More than three months away.'

So he knows too.

The main course arrives. I thank the waiter and gaze at the Challandais duck, poached quince and chestnut polenta with dismay. There appears to be too much on my plate. How on earth am I going to eat all this when I feel sick to my stomach?

'Bon appétit,' Marcus says and tucks into his escalopes de foie gras.

'Bon appétit,' Blake calls out to me.

'Bon appétit,' I mumble, duck, spice and honey on its way to my mouth.

When the table has been cleared Blake excuses himself, and rises from the table.

'Where are you going?' I ask in a panic.

He winks. 'I'll be back for you, babe.'

I watch him disappear out of sight before bringing my gaze back to Marcus. He is watching me. I smile weakly.

'So,' he says, leaning back in his chair. 'You caught a *very* big fish in your net. What will you do with it now?'

Eleven

'I don't know what you mean, and I resent both your tone and the implication that I have somehow trapped your brother.'

'What would you call it?'

'I *love* your brother.'

'You don't have to pretend with me. I don't care who my brother fucks. It's totally his business if he wants to take every little whore he comes across into his bed.'

'If you are that unconcerned, why do you ask?'

'Just curious,' he says and smiles pompously. At that moment he reminds me of his father, but less dangerous, by far less dangerous. I was afraid of his father, but I am not of him.

My mother's voice is quoting Rumi in my head. *You are searching in the branches for what is only in the roots.* Thank you, Mum. At that moment, I stop feeling inferior. Why should I? He is not more than me. I have done nothing wrong. He is the despicable one. By a quirk of fate he is thousands of times more privileged than 99.99 percent of the population, but that doesn't make him special or give him the right to treat everybody else as if they were beneath him.

'Please forgive me if I refuse to indulge your curiosity.' My voice is deadly calm.

He laughs. His eyes glitter. Malice shines in his face. 'Here's some free advice, sweetheart—Blake *will* tire of you. Start your going away fund right now.'

A waiter comes, removes Blake's used napkin and replaces it with a brand new napkin by carefully sliding it off the plate he had brought it in. He smiles and goes on his way unconcerned with the battle Marcus and I are engaged in.

'Why do you care if I am with Blake or not?'

'I told you I don't.'

He is lying. Of that I am sure. Will I unmask him? 'Ah, but you do.'

He raises his eyebrows, summons an expression of incredulity, but I am not fooled. I have love on my side.

'You're jealous,' I say. 'You're jealous of Blake and you are eaten up with envy because he has found something you don't have. You don't love anyone you'd give everything up for, do you?'

I see a flash of real anger in his eyes. Where is the studied carelessness now? He pretends to laugh, the sound unnatural, ugly. The façade is scratched, the mask slipping. Underneath the water the effortlessly gliding swan is kicking like crazy. He is nothing but a courtier. Trained by his father to put on a performance. Now he is lost to the façade he has put up. He is not to be reviled but pitied.

'Jealous?' he sneers.

I say nothing.

His voice becomes venomous. 'Of Blake?'

I maintain my silence. Keep eye contact.

'Because he has *you*? A two bit whore that he paid to acquire.' His voice is contemptuous.

'Love even in the arms of a two bit whore can be precious.'

'No thanks.'

From the corners of my eyes I see Blake walking towards us. I turn eagerly towards him. He is watching my face carefully.

'Everything all right?' he asks.

'Yes,' I answer, but my expression is stony. At that moment Alain Roux who is doing his customary tour of the dining room stops at our table. I smile stiffly and assure him that everything was wonderful. He nods graciously and moves on. I am ready to go home, but there is still the cheese trolley to endure.

Marcus pronounces the Auvergne cheese flawlessly 'kept', whatever that means.

Blake shrugs non-committally.

'How's your soufflé?' Marcus enquires, suave mask tightly in place.

I look him in the eye. 'Faultless.'

Marcus's smile does not reach his eyes. Mine slide over to Blake and he is smiling into his cheese. I spoon a mouthful of raspberry soufflé

into my mouth and know that I have won this round.

Blake orders a box of petits fours.

I look at him questioningly.

'For Billie,' he says and winks at me, and I feel a surge of joy. He is nothing like his brother. This horrible ordeal with Marcus is almost over and it will be just us again.

We say goodbye by Marcus's Bugatti Black Bess. Marcus shakes his brother's hand and touches his shoulder in an attempt to ingratiate himself with Blake. I stand apart and he does not attempt to kiss or touch me. I nod coldly—now you will have to win me over. Hands entwined we watch the lights of his car disappear into the darkness.

'I was proud of you tonight.'

'You left the table on purpose, didn't you?'

'Yes.'

'Why?'

'Because you have to get used to it. Marcus's disapproval is subtle and mild. If you can't hold your own with him, my mother will decimate you.'

'You're scaring me.'

He takes his eyes away from the darkness and focuses them on me. They are full of an emotion I cannot place. Maybe because, even though I love him with every ounce of my being, I don't know him well enough. Maybe because I am a fool in love with a man I cannot understand.

All I know is I love him no matter what.

'I'm preparing you. I wish I could always be by your side to protect you, but I can't. You must

learn to fend for yourself. You must realize on your own that they are nothing. You are better than all of them put together.'

I break eye contact and look down at my hands. I am the girl from the council estate. I won tonight, but with great difficulty.

'Be confident, my love. Don't ever ask for their approval or work for it. They will respect you more for it. You will never be one of them, but that's OK. I'd hate it if you were.'

'Are all of them going to be hateful to me, then?'

'They won't dare say anything while I am around, but you'll have to learn to handle the odd catty remark in my absence.'

'Right.'

'Marcus looked like a whipped dog when I came back to the table.'

'He did?'

He grins wolfishly. 'Absolutely.'

I smile but I am thinking of the woman in black who stood next to Blake at the funeral. I know he is her favorite son and she will hate me with a passion. 'When am I meeting your mother?'

He laughs. 'We'll avoid that torture for as long as possible.'

'She's going to hate me, isn't she?'

'Yes. But as the two of you will hardly ever meet that shouldn't bother you at all.'

I sigh loudly. 'They all want you to be with Victoria.'

'That's never going to happen and it's time they got used to it.'

I thrust the box of petits fours into Billie's stomach and she opens it immediately. Blake goes on into Sorab's room, and I stand talking to her as she eats the sweets and looks at me with shrewd eyes.

'Anything to tell me?' she whispers as soon as Blake is out of earshot.

'Tell you tomorrow.'

She nods. 'Mmmmm... These are delicious.'

I reach out and brush a crumb from the corner of her lips. 'God, Billie, how I love you.'

'You should go out to dinner more often with Marcus,' she says.

And for the first time that night I laugh.

Twelve

I look down at my sleeping son and savor the delicious pleasure of his warm weight in my lap. I stroke his downy head. So exposed, so vulnerable. I feel Blake's eyes on me and look up at him. He is looking at both of us with an expression that I can only describe as fierce pride and possession. I feel cocooned in that savage light. As long as he is around we will both be safe.

Blake settles Sorab in his cot while I get out of my dress. I hang it up carefully and start removing my make-up. I don't take off my new jewelry. Blake loves to have me wearing nothing but the jewelry he has put on my body. I brush my hair and teeth, wrap myself in a fluffy bathrobe—it is deliciously warm from the radiator—and go out into the bedroom. He is unbuttoning his shirt. He pulls the ends out of his trousers.

'Come here,' he says.

I go up to him.

'Have I told you how beautiful you looked tonight?'

I nod.

'Have I told you how proud I was of you tonight?'

I nod.

'Hmmnnn... I am in danger of being boring.'

'I love boring men.'

One end of his lips curve.

'Whoa... High alert... Edible sexy ahead,' I whisper.

'Serve warm, eat whole,' he says as his hands move to the belt on my robe. He undoes it deftly and slowly leans into the gaping material to plant a kiss on my right nipple. My heart starts crashing against my chest. His large hands disappear inside the folds of the material and slide sensuously down the sides of my body. They come to a stop at my hips. He squeezes.

'Amazing how I never tire of looking at your body,' he murmurs into the side of my neck, while his fingers caress my throat and the blue stones encircling it.

The robe drops off, my head drops back. A trail of kisses follows. A small sound escapes my throat. Amazing how my body quivers like jelly as soon as he touches me. His hands grasp my wrists and pull them upwards until they are held high above my head.

He holds my wrists in a potent grasp with one hand and looks down at me, while his other hand roams my body freely, possessively. As if I am a slave in an auction that he is considering buying. I look up into his eyes. They are bold and dominant. I let my lips part.

'My Jezebel,' he says huskily, and takes my lower lip between his teeth. He holds the plump flesh between his teeth and pulls so I am forced to move with his head. I stand on tiptoe, skin burning all over, and wet between the legs. He lets go of my lip and moving his dark head away from me, gazes down at my body, arched and stretched out in front of him. There is a look of great satisfaction on his face.

He turns me around. 'Hands on the bed.'

I open my legs, bend over, and put my palms on the bed, shoulder width apart, waist dipped down, ass high in the air. I know what he is doing. He is making me wait.

Anticipation.

I twist my head and watch him unhurriedly shrug out of his shirt, very deliberately pull the belt out of his trouser loops, release the button at the top of the zip, pull down the zip. Hook his fingers inside his underpants. Pull down. He stands behind me. Hot, hard, ready. I watch his glorious body eagerly.

'Who do you belong to?' he purrs.

'You.' My voice is hoarse.

'Which parts belong to me?'

'All.'

'All?'

'All.'

He kneels behind me, his face inches from my sex.

'I can smell your arousal,' he says.

I shut my eyes. I am so open, so exposed. Seconds drip by. I wait. I know it's all a game. Patience and anticipation. My skin prickles. I feel his hot breath fan my wet flesh. The shock of his silky tongue swirling between the swollen folds makes my head jerk back. Instinctively, my hips tilt upwards, in a begging posture. I need him inside me. Now.

'Please, Blake. Please. Enter me.'

'Is this mine?' he asks, and bites my sex.

'Arggg...'

'I'm sorry,' he says pleasantly. 'I couldn't make that out.' He bites me again.

'Yes,' I cry out.

'To do with as I please?'

'Yes, yes.'

His breath fans the flushed, sensitized skin. With his thumbs, he spreads apart the folds and inserts his tongue. I gasp and writhe. He pulls my thighs farther apart, clamps his mouth on my clit and sucks.

'Oh God!'

Just as the delicious waves are starting to take hold, he takes his mouth away. Torture, pure torture. He stands. Is there to be no filling, stretching, or ramming? I am raging with need. To have him deep inside me. To be possessed by him. Frustrated and full of longing I look at him. Silently, he is gazing down at my open, greedy pussy.

'Stay,' he says, and leaving my body, gets on the bed in front of me. I gaze at his erection. My mouth

is open, my breathing erratic. He is a fine specimen of a man. I have the strong urge to lick the meatus, take him in my mouth, and suck him so hard he groans helplessly.

But he has an even better idea.

'Come and sit on my cock,' he commands.

The order rolls over my flesh. I don't need a second invitation. I crawl to him and impale myself on the hard shaft. The pleasure. Oh! the pleasure.

'Sit like a frog.'

I reposition myself, opening my knees wide, pulling my feet close to his thighs and laying them flat on the bed. Then I place my palms on his body and straighten my own body. The penetration is too deep. With a small cry I push my palms down and fractionally lift myself off his body, but he shakes his head slowly.

'Mine to do with as I please.'

Biting my lip I relax my arms and let my body take the whole shaft, gasping at the sudden pain. For a while he makes me endure it, the sensation of being too full, the exquisite pain of having him too deep inside me.

'Your pussy feels so fucking good I could stay inside you all night.'

We stare at each other. My eyes must be full of wonder. His blaze with the excitement of dominating me, seeing me in that crouched position, my thighs wide open, his cock buried so deep inside my body I can barely bear it. I whimper, and he takes pity on me.

'Lean forward,' he growls softly.

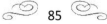

Immediately I obey, and the pain goes away. All that remains is the pure pleasure of being stretched and filled to the brim. He pushes my breasts inwards and pulling me towards him sucks hard at my nipple, first one then the other. I start to move against his shaft and we groan in unison. My clit rubs against his pubic bone. Back and forth. Back and forth, as far as his greedily sucking mouth will allow me to retreat to. Rubbing. Rubbing. Delicious friction. Our bodies become wet and slippery. It is beautiful.

He waits for me to come before he allows himself to erupt inside me. I collapse on him and lay my cheek upon his chest. I can hear the fast, dull thudding of his heart, and feel his strong shaft still jerking inside me. I lift my head. His eyes are closed, his face is calm.

'Are you sleepy?' I ask.

'No.'

I use the ends of my hair to tickle his chin. 'What's your favorite word?'

He opens his eyes. 'Egg.'

'What?'

'I just like the sound of it.'

'You're one strange man.'

He chuckles. 'What's yours?'

'Lollipop.'

'I'd like to change my word.'

'To what?'

'Lana.'

I laugh. 'That, Mr. Barrington, is the corniest thing you have ever said to me.'

'No, really. Every time I say it, or hear it on someone else's lips, it actually gives me a thrill.'

I feel lazy and relaxed on top of him. 'We know so little about each other, don't we?'

'I know everything I need to know about you. Everything else I'll find out along the way.'

'What is it you think you know about me?'

'Well, for starters I know you're brave.'

I frown. 'Brave? I'm not brave.'

'You're one of the bravest people I know.'

'How am I brave?'

'You left me. That's brave.'

'If you knew how frightened and confused I was when I left.'

'That's the definition of bravery, Lana. Doing something even though you are terrified of the consequences. And I am really proud of the way you handled my brother today, too.'

'You are?' I squeak, immeasurably pleased with the compliment.

'When I was in the toilet I was so nervous about leaving you with him I was gripping the edges of the sink to keep from running back into the restaurant. But I knew I had to let you handle it, and I'm glad now that I did. If you can handle him you can handle all the rest in time.'

'I hope you're right.'

'And if I'm not we'll work it out together.'

Thirteen

Victoria Montgomery

If I had a flower for every time I thought of you...
I could walk through my garden forever,

Alfred Tennyson

This morning he calls me and tells me he is coming to see me. He sounds puzzlingly distant, but still, I sense that he is desperate to see me again. Finally. I never once—well, maybe once or twice—doubted that he would tire of that thieving bitch. I've always known—he will come back.

I look at the clock. He'll be here in less than an hour! Feeling almost dizzy with excitement and triumph, I slip into white underwear. The silk slides deliciously against my fevered skin. Blake loves a woman in white. The slut knew that, too. Her underwear drawers were full of white bits and pieces. My lips tighten of their own accord. I won't think of her now. Why should I? I've won.

I, too, can drive him crazy with need. I, too, can slowly strip and crawl on the floor towards him. I will unzip his trousers and take his thick manhood, throbbing with power and strength, deep into my throat. I will swallow what he gives me. He is *my* man. I will be Mrs. Blake Law Barrington. I will walk into restaurants and parties and people will see that I am the power behind the throne.

I look at myself in the long mirror and don't just feel reassured and satisfied, but highly pleased with the image that looks back. If there is a woman more desirable than me then I am yet to meet her. I am a class act all the way. That woman—I cannot even bear to say her name—is cheap. Even the best designer clothes cannot hide that fact. It lurks in her eyes, her big lips, her silly butter wouldn't melt in my mouth expression.

I dress simply in a mint green dress, its hem faultlessly grazing the tops of my knees. I encircle my throat with two rows of creamy pearls. Nothing elaborate. It wouldn't be appropriate to display my triumph. Some decorum and subtlety is called for. And yet this dress knows how to ride up my thighs when I sit down. Maybe... He will slide his hand up the inside of my thigh and, moving aside my knickers, insert his strong fingers into me, one, two, maybe even three... Forcing them deeper and deeper, working them furiously, until I gasp. Until I come, drenching his hand.

I imagine him pushing my dress up so it bunches around my waist. He will roughly tear away my knickers, open my long, slender legs wide, and while I arch my spine with uncontrollable lust, he will eat me out like a wild beast. And I will hold him by the hair until... I climax again.

'You taste so much better than her,' he will say to me.

My legs are trembling and my knickers are wet. I push a finger into my own wet hole, and pulling it out put it into my mouth. This is me. That is what he will taste. Then a thought: You don't have much time. I snap out of my fantasy. I must be the picture of calm loyalty.

Quickly, I move to my dressing table.

Nearly black mascara, smoky brown eyeshadow and luscious berry lipstick. I press my lips together, and let the color pigments spread. Nice. Very nice. I'll just be soft and innocent. That always works. I dab perfume—potent and specially created for me—behind my ears, on the insides of my wrists and then a strip on the insides of my thighs. I do not change out of my wet knickers. I actually relish the thought of sitting next to him, wet. Maybe he will smell me.

For an instant I consider changing into something more revealing.

The soft peal of the doorbell stops me cold for a second. Too late. Mint green will have to do. I lay my palm on my stomach. I am as nervous as I was on our first date. What a night that was. We dined

90

at Nobu and ended up at a party. How happy I was then. Everywhere we went people looked at us with envy. We were the golden couple.

I take a deep, steadying breath and walk to the door. My footfalls are light and noiseless on the thick carpet. With each step I become calmer, more clear in my purpose. I open the door smiling softly, knowing I am looking my best, and my face is radiant with the pure love I have for him.

'Hello Victoria,' he says politely.

His eyes. His eyes. So flat and cold. He has changed. He has changed. The rush from heaven to hell is dizzying. I am overwhelmed with grief as one is after a death. I take Blake's hand and, bending one knee in a gesture of respect reserved only for the highest ranking leaders, kiss it.

'Don't,' he grates harshly, yanking his hand away. 'I am not my father.'

Confused and slightly unsteady, I rise. How different he is.

'Please come in.' I let the door yawn wider and he steps through. I can do this. He stands awkwardly in my hallway. I turn away from him and close the door. My heart is breaking. Has that fucking bitch poisoned him against me?

'Let's have some tea,' I say, turning to face him. My eyes are schooled, innocent, seemingly totally unaware of what he has been doing with the *slut.*

He seems about to say something, changes his mind, and nods. I had raised my victory flag too early. I have not won yet. He does not want to be here. He does not want me. I keep my expression neutral, friendly. We go into the living room where a sumptuous tea is waiting. As we enter the living room, I see Maria, my housekeeper, slip out of the front door.

I indicate the divan and we sit next to each other. Tia, my solid chocolate Persian, poses on her chair across from us. My eyes graze the thigh next to mine. Under the fine wool it is sculptured with hard muscles. I have seen the photographs. I grasp the teapot and pour tea into two cups. I know exactly how he likes his—black, two sugars.

'Milk?' I ask.

'Black.'

'Sugar?'

'Two please.'

He watches me as I drop two sugar cubes into his tea. I hold it out to him. I am dying to touch the shapely, masculine fingers, but I don't. He takes the saucer by its lip, far away from my fingers. I raise my eyes towards him and take a small sip of my tea—milk, no sugar.

'I'm sorry about your father. He was a good man.' I smile sadly at him. I don't have to pretend sorrow. The death of his father is a great, great blow to me. He was an ally, a very powerful ally. A friend I could trust with my back. One who shared the same goal. But he is gone now.

'Thank you.' His voice is far away.

'And now you are the head of the Barrington fortune.'

He frowns. It makes him look commanding.

I reach for a gold-rimmed plate of fruitcake. Since he was a boy he never could resist fruitcake. I had these specially ordered from my father's chef. 'Would you like a slice?'

'Thank you.'

I watch him bite into it. He is perfect. From the bold, hard slash of his mouth to the taut cheekbones to his naturally bronze coloring, to the dark hair, he is perfect. He is my heart. He is mine. The thought is fiercely possessive and feels right. I must have him or I will die.

I reach under the white muslin for a scone. It is still warm. I butter it, spread a thin layer of jam, bring it to my mouth, and realize I will be sick if it passes my lips. But he is watching me with the narrowed eyes of a predator. Narrowed and assessing. What is he thinking? I have photos of him when he is with that ridiculous woman, when his eyes are caressing and infinitely tender. I take a small bite, chew until I can no longer bear it in my mouth, and swallow. A mouthful of tea makes it go down.

'Look, I might as well come clean right away. I've fallen in love with Lana,' he announces abruptly.

Fourteen

I think my eyes widen. From the moment I met his cold, dead eyes at the front door I had been expecting such a declaration, but my reaction was involuntary. Simply couldn't help it. Hearing the harshness of his words. No 'Sorry I wasted your fucking time. Sorry I led you on a merry dance all these years. Sorry I irreparably shattered your heart into a thousand sharp shards.' Nothing. Just that arrow right into my heart. A sick fury rises inside me. The fury of being denied, deprived. When I was two I didn't throw myself on the ground in a tantrum, I used to run to the servants and kick and punch them hard. Until the fury was appeased and abated. I cannot show him that rage. I lower my eyes quickly.

'I'm really sorry,' he says.

His voice is gentle, but when I look up at him, his eyes are watchful, utterly, utterly unrepentant and full of the realization of how foolish the idea of marrying me was. How could he ever have thought he could marry me and play house?

'She doesn't understand our ways. She won't have the stomach to do the *necessary* things.'

A veil comes over his eyes. 'I don't want her to do any of those things. I want to keep her out of all that. We will be a normal family.'

'But you have taken the vow.'

'The only vow I have taken is silence. And I won't break that.'

'From the path thou shall not stray.'

'I already have.'

I frown. 'You'd give up ultimate power for her?'

He smiles sadly. 'Oh, Victoria. How little you know me. I was not even going to ask you to do those things. I don't want the power. I detest what we are doing. I went along because I didn't know any better. Let the others fight it out for the ultimate power. The only reason I remain is because leaving is not an option.'

I reach out a hand and touch his sleeve and... He recoils. Imperceptibly, but it is there. An inhuman claw inside my chest squeezes tighter and tighter until I feel I almost cannot breathe at all. So this also is love, I reflect with wonder. No one can imagine just how poisonous is the hate in my heart for that beastly woman who stole my man.

Lana fucking Bloom.

She had no right. I rock with helpless pain.

Instantly, he reaches for my hand. It is satiny soft, but icy and quite lifeless.

'Are you all right?' His voice seems muffled, as if he is talking to me while I am under water.

I nod. I must gather myself. I can still turn this around. I take a deep breath, stop rocking, and, dry-eyed, turn to look at him.

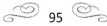

'Are you sure you're all right?' he repeats.

I fix a bright smile on my lips. 'Of course.'

'You deserve to find someone who will love you. We didn't love each other. We were marrying for all the wrong reasons. I know that now,' he says with breathtaking masculine selfishness.

Yes, you found your slut and now you just want to push me away. I recall again how I had decided to offer myself to him when he called me this morning. To show him how good we'd be together.

I nod. 'You are right. This is probably for the best. We would probably have ended up in the divorce courts.' I smile again. Conciliatory.

He reciprocates with a smile of his own. He thinks it is all over. Just like that he can wash his hands of me.

'You have a son?'

Twin lights blossom in his eyes. If he takes out his wallet and shows me a picture of their blasted baby, I swear, I will scream, but he doesn't.

'He's the joy of my life,' he says simply.

In those few words I see a world I can never have. In my head a voice is sneering, 'Resentment is like drinking poison and waiting for the other person to die.' Of their own accord my delicate fingers start drumming dangerously on the glass-topped coffee table. I see his eyes shift to my hand. I jerk it away and clasp it in my other hand. I need to do something quickly. He is fixing to leave. I swallow hard at the lump in my throat and stare at the glass surface. How insidiously smooth and unyielding it is. My vision takes in the edge of the plate with the uneaten scone, the butter knife... It is sheer madness, I could even put my eye out, but in a split second I make my decision.

I let my body pitch forward as if my bones have suddenly melted. The smooth hard glass, the knife's gleaming blade, and sharp edge of the table rise up to meet my face. Anybody else would have halted their fall, saved themselves, given in to the instinct to protect themselves. I didn't.

And what a good thing that I was brave.

I risked gouging out my eye and won. Just inches away from the pointed end of the knife, hard hands catch me by the arms. I am bodily lifted and held close to his body, the scent of him assailing my senses. God, I love this man so much. I keep my eyes closed, my body limp and floppy. My dress has ridden up my thighs.

'Victoria,' Blake calls urgently, but I allow my neck to droop over his arms, so my throat is bared to him and he can savor the vulnerability of my lifeless limbs in his arms. Let him feel masculine and strong and protective. The position is awkward and he stands lifting me up with him. It is unexpectedly and deliciously romantic, and I feel like one of those women on the jacket covers of the voluptuous romances my mother reads.

I wish he could hold me like this forever, but he lays me back on the divan. However, he is so gentle about it that I suddenly realize he must love me. He doesn't know it, but it is I who am the one he truly loves. He must just use her for sex. It is me that he loves. Always me. He pulls my dress down

over my thighs. What a gentleman. He could have taken advantage of me. Peeked at my sex. Or even had sex with my inert body.

That is a great fantasy of mine.

That I would lie on a table as if in a swoon and a total stranger, someone dark and dangerous, someone like Blake, would come and roughly thrust my thighs open, and fuck my plump little sex mercilessly, painfully. I would feel everything, but I would be unable to make a single sound of protest as his enormous organ would split me remorselessly.

But as the man realizes how hungry and wet I am for him, he understands that I crave the thorough use of my body. Then he becomes sublimely cruel. My own silence deafens me. I weep silently as he does terrible things to me. Until I am hardly human. Afterwards, he will leave even before I wake up.

Sometimes I would even fantasize that a group of men come, all colors and scents, to use my body while I am lying there. None of them would use condoms. They would use every orifice. They would speak of me as if I was nothing but a piece of meat.

Blake is sliding his hands away from under the backs of my knees and my neck and I sense him standing. Seconds later my head is lifted and a cushion placed under it. I hear him striding towards the bathroom. He returns with a cold face towel that he lays on my forehead. I moan softly and allow my eyelids to flutter slightly. He calls my name. I open my eyes and allow them to roll a little.

'What happened?' I ask weakly.

'You fainted.'

I attempt to rise to my elbows, then pretend as if the effort is making me dizzy. My head sways unsteadily.

'Take it easy. Lie back down.'

I let myself fall back with a sigh. I look up at him. He is frowning.

'Does this happen often?' he asks.

I shake my head. 'I'll be fine in a minute.'

'Can I get you anything?'

'I feel cold.'

He looks around and, seeing nothing with which to cover me, takes off his jacket and lays it on my upper body. The warmth of his body lingers and I just want to close my eyes and savor it. Oh, why, oh why did she come and steal him away from me? Everything was going fine until she came into the picture. He loves me really. We are not strangers. We have grown up together.

'I'm sorry,' he says softly.

I know he is. It is that filthy bitch who has him all tied up with sex. I should have slept with him, I would have him now. My heart is full of bitter regret that I never slept with him.

'It's not your fault,' I whisper. Tears begin to flow from my eyes.

He kneels beside me.

'Do you know what I regret the most?'

'No.'

'I regret that we never made love, even once. Can we? Just once. For old times sake?'

My tears dry as suddenly as they began. I look up at him through damp lashes. He is staring at me without revealing any emotion, but my heart and my eyes are full of hot, hungry craving for him. My whole being is on fire for him. Right then all I want is to feel his burning lips on my lips, face, throat, breasts, between my legs...until I am driven out of my mind. I snake my tongue out, run it along my lower lip.

'Just this once.' My voice is husky and thick, my eyes half-hooded.

He is still staring at me sans expression, so I bend my head so my hair parts and exposes the defenseless white curve that is the nape of my neck. For a moment Blake makes neither move nor response, until unexpectedly, in the downcast line of my vision, I see his leather shoes quietly turn away from me. And start to head towards the door. He is leaving. He is actually going.

The bastard!

For a precious few seconds I lie shocked, silent and paralyzed, the blood running cold in my veins. Even my brain refuses to think. It never, never occurred to me that he could simply walk away from me. What now?

Then I stand and call him.

He doesn't stop.

My stomach lurches. 'You can't leave me.'

He stops and turns around to face me. His laughter rings hollow, rasping and devoid of

 100

humor. 'You see something you want, you just reach out and take it, don't you?'

'You're a fine one to talk,' I retort. Shit I shouldn't have said that. I stare at him in a panic. It has all gone so wrong.

'You're so fucking spoilt.' His words do not match his eyes, though. They are weary, the eyes of a man who has had enough. He shakes his head and starts walking away from me. He is already at the door. His hand is reaching for the handle. And suddenly I know. I know exactly how to stop him in his tracks. And I know how to make it convincing, too. I take a rush of air into my lungs.

'I know what it tastes like. I've taken part,' I cry out. My voice is like a bell in the silent room.

His hand freezes. He turns slowly. 'What?'

Fifteen

His expression is one of great shock. My father is not a lowly member to offer his daughter in such a way. There is a seed of distrust in his eyes, and yet there is compassion and softness. She has changed him. I have never seen this look in his eyes.

'I was just a child. I never made a sound. I never saw their faces. They took turns. I can never forget,' I whisper. I am a convincing actress.

He strides over to me and puts his arms around me. 'I'm sorry, Victoria. So sorry. I didn't know. He should have protected you.'

'It doesn't matter now. I just wanted you to know that I've suffered too.'

'I didn't plan it this way,' he says softly. 'It just happened. I fell in love with her.'

I look up at him with great, big eyes. 'I'm not blaming you for falling in love with another woman. I'm not even angry with you or her. But I am hurting. Real bad. It's simple for you. "Let's be friends," you say, but it's not so easy for me. I love you. I always have and I always will. It's inside me, day and night eating at me relentlessly. My heart is

102

bleeding, Blake. I can't eat. I can't sleep. I know you didn't ask for my heart, but I gave it, anyway.' I smile bitterly. 'You'd be shocked if you knew how much I hurt. I feel as if I am going mad.'

He looks into my eyes, saddened, incredibly so. 'Oh, Victoria.'

'The heart was meant to be broken,' I say, quoting Oscar Wilde. I know he will recognize and smile.

He half smiles. 'I didn't know it was like that for you. I don't know what I thought. These arrangements,' he opens his palms out helplessly, 'they are not meant to be like this.' He stops for a moment. 'I didn't think because I didn't care for you, for me, or anyone else for that matter. I was a brute.'

'Welcome to my world,' I say.

I can see that he pities me.

'I have to go,' he mutters.

'Look after my heart. You hold it in your hand.'

He kisses the top of my head and then he is gone, shutting the door quietly behind him.

'I prayed for you,' I whisper at the closed door.

How long I stood staring at the door, utterly devastated and uncomprehending, my dreams and hopes scattered around me, I don't know. Perhaps I thought he might still return. Ring the bell and come in, tell me it has all been a dreadful mistake. I even waited past the obligatory one hundred and eighty seconds while my mind replayed the humiliation of my total rejection. I only really come to when I feel silky fur rubbing against my bare legs. I look down. Tia purrs gently.

I bend down and pick up her warm, soft body. I press her pliant silkiness against my chest and look into her beautiful face. She stares at me with her one blue and one copper eye, blinks and tries to snuggle up between my breasts. Even the cat has found contentment in its life.

Without warning that intense hot bubble of poison that is always lying in wait in the very depths of my bowels shoots sickeningly into my head. It explodes in a shower of red-hot sparks right between my eyes. As if hit by lightning I react. I lose it. Go ape-shit crazy. With a wild cry of fury and with all the viciousness of a female cobra on a nest of unhatched eggs, I hurl the unsuspecting cat against the wall. She crashes into the wall in a screaming confusion of distended nails and flying fur. The animal rights itself, curses, spits and hisses at me before fleeing in a chocolate streak of confused terror and pain.

My curled nails bite deeply into my own flesh, but I feel no pain, only the need to destroy. I turn and look at myself in the mirrored wall. My face is flushed and blazing with color, my eyes are savage, my mouth is open and breathing hard as if I have been running, and my breasts are heaving.

Something sick swirls in my stomach. My heart begins to race. I hear a rattling in my head and my mouth fills with the taste of metal. I feel the tremble begin in my fingers. It's happening. At first slight, so slight it is like the shaking of an alcoholic in the morning before his first drink. But it becomes stronger, more insistent. I let it. It is a fine feeling. The way it sweeps into my body, takes over and becomes a roaring ball of pure energy.

The room in front of me swirls slightly. Objects come into focus, lose their edges and come back into being. My trembling body begins to shake violently. Suddenly, I am sucked into a vortex of energy and I feel myself flying across the room. I grab a bespoke dining chair as if it weighed nothing more than a matchstick, raise it high over my head, and running to the mirrored wall slam it against the surface. The sound of exploding glass is loud, satisfying. Again. And again. The chair breaks. I see myself in the broken mirror. Galvanized, I am indeed a terrible vision, flying hair, bared teeth.

I destroy everything!

Eventually when I fall down in an exhausted heap on the floor, the room is in total shambles. The expensive brocade curtains lie in shreds, every breakable thing accuses me in shattered silence and my beautiful nails are torn and bleeding. My eyes travel over the destruction I have wreaked, but I find no remorse in my heart. I am filled only with defiance.

As a matter of fact, I feel much better now. It's been refreshing and deeply cleansing to damage so indiscriminately. Tomorrow, I will go shopping. And shopping always gives me a fantastic boost. I will get something nice for Tia (I shouldn't have flung her against the wall) and something stunningly expensive and beautiful for me, for when Blake comes back to me. This is just a minor setback. Obviously, he will tire of her.

I stand. A sharp pain tears through my knee. I look down.

A huge bruise is coming up. The hem of my dress is torn too. I limp over to the bathroom and stand in front of the mirror. I gaze at myself. Moisture-filled luminous eyes in a pale face. I realize anew that I really am extraordinarily beautiful. I pout at my own reflection. Transfixed by my own beauty I form words, just to watch my berry lips in movement. Quite of their own volition they say, 'I'll get him back. Of course I will.'

Sixteen

Lana Bloom

I have spent most of the day on the phone with lawyers and advisors discussing the best way for me to set up and run my charity. Now I am in the kitchen making a simple dinner while Sorab is napping inside his playpen. When Blake comes home I don't rush out to the front door because the asparagus will be ready in less than a minute and I don't want to overcook it.

'We're in the kitchen,' I call out, keeping my voice fairly soft in order not to wake Sorab.

I hear Blake close the front door. He appears in the doorway, leans against it and simply looks at me.

'What is it?'

He just shakes his head and continues gazing at me.

'Blake?'

To my horror his eyes fill with tears.

I put down the colander of asparagus and run to him.

I put my fingers on his damp lashes. 'Oh, my darling, what's wrong?'

He catches my fingers in his hand and presses them against his lips. 'Nothing. I am just drinking in the sight of you.'

His lips turn into a soft kiss on my fingertips. He sweeps his hand along my jaw line.

'That's a good thing, right?' I joke.

'I love you, Lana. I never stop thinking of you. Never. The only thing I am afraid of in this life is losing you. You know I'd risk everything for you, don't you?'

Warmth starts spreading throughout my body. 'I am right here, Blake. Where I belong, where I'll always be.'

'I went to see Victoria today.'

'Oh.'

'I told her I'm in love with you.'

'How did she react?'

'She fell apart. I did not expect it. She was pitiful.'

I move slightly away from him. 'It was not your father who paid me to leave. It was her.'

'I know. When I found out that Sorab was mine, I traced the money through its complicated trusts back to her. I was furious—she had caused me a year of excruciating pain—but confronting her was not a priority. All information is power, and everything I knew, and my opponent thought I did not was my advantage. So I never revealed my hand or acted on the knowledge.

 108

'When I went to see her today I was prepared to coldly dismiss her from our lives, but then she said something which made me pity her. The truth is, I did lead her on. I did renege on my promise to marry her. She has some grounds for her anger and suffering. I never wanted revenge and now I actually pity her. I have everything. She has nothing. I wish her well. One day I hope we will be friends.'

'She didn't seem pitiful to me.'

'She is the spoilt daughter of a very wealthy man and she is used to getting what she wants, but even she has been broken by love. She will no longer trouble us.'

I say nothing.

That evening Sorab falls asleep on top of his father's body in the living room. I follow to watch as Blake tucks Sorab in for the night. First Blake, and then I bend to kiss his smooth cheek as he lies asleep on his side. When I raise my eyes to Blake's he is watching me. In the shadows and soft light of the bedroom he looks proudly proprietorial. We are his family.

He comes around the cot, takes me by the hand, leads me into our bedroom...and makes love to me, as he has never done before. With infinite gentleness as if I am a delicate butterfly whose wings can come off as dust pigments on his fingers, if he does not take the greatest care in the way he handles me. All of it is long, or slow, or deep, and when he climaxes he calls my name as if he is falling off a cliff and I am the last thing he sees. The longing in his voice is a balm to my heart.

I stretch luxuriously and lie on my stomach.

He lets his fingers run up and down my spine. 'I love the feel of your spine, the delicate little bones that make your body. They are like skin-covered teeth, only they are not. As you move they flow under my fingers.'

I chuckle. 'Oh my God! We have unearthed the poet in you.'

'It's love. The loved destroys the thing that loves it.'

I turn around to face him, a frown etched on my brow. 'Are you saying your love for me is destroying you?'

He cups my naked breast possessively. 'The more I love you the more of a stranger I have become to myself. Now I do and say things that I would never have dreamed of doing or saying. I can hardly believe that I lived all these years without you.'

I run my finger down his cheek. 'Sometimes I get so scared. Everything I have ever loved has been taken away from me.' I look down to the duvet cover. My voice trembles like the strings of a harp. I bite back the tears that have so suddenly arrived to spoil what should have been a beautiful moment.

He leans in and kisses the top of my left shoulder. 'My love, my love, if you are still living and I am not, then I will haunt you until your dying day.'

I look up at him with hurt eyes. 'That's not funny, Barrington.'

'I know, my darling heart. It's only funny in the fucked up world I exist in. The real truth is, I want us to be like those ancient couples who have never been apart a day in their lives and when one partner dies the other follows in hours.'

'Me too. I even hate saying goodnight to you. It means I'll lose you again for a few more hours.'

He puts a finger against my temple. 'Sometimes I wake up and watch you sleeping.'

'Oh.'

'Do you know you sometimes smile in your sleep?'

'I do?'

'You always look so defenseless and angelic, like one of those fairy princesses from my childhood days.'

'A fairy princess?' I love the idea.

'Yes, often I wish I could lock you away in an enchanted tower. Nobody could get to you except me.'

'You don't have to look me away in a tower. I'm always here for you.'

'The princess is not locked up because she is bad. The princess is locked up because she is precious beyond words, and everyone wants a piece of her.' His voice changes, becomes serious. 'I have to put you somewhere you can't be hurt.'

'I am at that somewhere. Right here, beside you.'

He frowns. 'But when I am not around—'

'Brian and his pack take over.'

'I'd still prefer to lock you up in an enchanted tower.'

'That doesn't sound quite fair. I get locked up while you go into the world and do all the things that you love to do.'

'I don't love what I do, Lana. I do it because I have to.'

'Why can't you walk away? You have more than we can ever spend.'

'Sometimes we are given the illusion of choice. Give a man dying of thirst in a desert a glass of water and tell him it's his choice. Drink or leave it. Is that really a choice, Lana?'

I say nothing. I remember when my mother was so ill that choice became an illusion.

'I am like that man,' he continues. 'If I drink it will mean danger to you and Sorab. I know too much for them to allow me to walk away. I have responsibilities that I must see through.'

'Responsibilities to carry on destroying the world?'

He smiles sadly and puts his finger on my lips. 'No more. That will happen with or without me.'

'Then why do you have to do it?'

'What happens to the whistleblower, Lana?'

'They get put in prison or they or their loved ones meet with "accidents" or they commit "suicide" and the agenda goes on uninterrupted.'

I frown and move my mouth away from his finger. 'Why—?'

His fingers stop my lips, stop any further conversation. His eyes look so sad I wish I had never started this conversation. I move towards him and hug him hard. He is in pain. Terrible pain, but he cannot tell me. He is the man in the desert with a glass full of cool, life-giving water. I am asking him to drink, but he is resisting because of me and Sorab. I realize then that he has reason for the secrecy he maintains. He believes it is for the greater good. He believes harm will befall me and Sorab. I have to accept it. I decide then to stop pestering him. I will do my own research.

'I'm going to church tomorrow.'

'OK, what time would you like us to go?'

I stare at him, astonished. 'You mean you'll come to church with me?'

He shrugs. 'Sure why not?'

'But what about the brotherhood?'

'The cloak of respectability the brotherhood wears is organized religion.'

And I remember that his father's funeral had been held in a church. 'But if you come with me, wouldn't that be a sham?'

He looks me in the eye. 'No, it wouldn't.'

'I'm going to love you like I'll never be hurt.'

He lays his head on the pillow beside me and looks deep into my eyes. 'Often I look at you and I can't believe my luck,' he whispers.

Two days later I am pushing Sorab on High Street Kensington when time suddenly suspends. The blood stills in my veins. For a moment it is as if I am in a movie frame that suddenly freezes.

Victoria is standing only a few yards away. We stare at each other. Her eyes are translucent with a strange mixture of bewilderment and hatred. She reminds me of a wild animal that is caught in a mangle. It is dangerous because it is so desperate. I know I am safe—Brian is only a shout away—but I still feel the icy claw of fear squeeze at my heart.

She takes a step towards me and my internal organs lurch as if I am in a fast-moving lift that suddenly stops. My mind instantly starts making plans to protect Sorab. A voice in my brain says, 'She wouldn't dare,' but I stand ready.

She begins to walk towards me, her head held straight, but her eyes unblinking and deadly are trained on me, the eyeballs moving to the sides of her eyes as she passes by me. So close to me, almost her shoulder brushing mine. The malice and madness I see in her eyes chill me to the bone. And yet, she has done nothing. I turn around and watch her walk away without once turning back.

I clamp my hand over my mouth, as if to cover the horror of the knowledge that she has fooled Blake. She will be trouble. But how will I convince him otherwise? She has done nothing to me.

That night Blake's lips crash against mine, and afterwards he tells me we are going to Dubai—a romantic weekend. I lose myself in the moment and forget the maniacal hatred in Victoria's eyes...momentarily.

Seventeen

When we arrive at the airport I am surprised to note that we are not getting into Blake's Gulfstream jet, but a Boeing 767. We walk through the doors and I gawp in awed silence. It looks like no plane I've ever been in. Brand new and customized to look like the interior of an apartment it is luxurious and stunningly elegant.

I turn to Blake. 'Do you own this?'

'It's registered to the Bank of Utah.'

'But really it's yours?'

He shrugs. 'Own nothing, control everything.'

Smiling staff come forth with smiles and hot towels.

After take-off I turn to Blake. 'Can I explore?'

'Want me to show you?'

'Nope. Want to take it all in on my own.'

He smiles and reaches for his briefcase. 'Knock yourself out.'

I touch my lips to his. 'I will.'

I take Sorab from Jerry and we start exploring the three floors. It is truly amazing. All the spaces have no hard edges, everything curves and swirls around to meet the next environment. There is a dining table that seats twenty, three guest bedroom suites, lifts, a kitchen, an office, a boardroom, two sumptuous lounges with cream couches, a concert hall, a TV room, a gym and a sauna.

We end up in the master bedroom, which is on two levels. I playfully throw Sorab on the massive white bed and he bounces and squeals with startled laughter. He lifts his hands up to me. I pick him up and throw him back down on the bed. He laughs happily and lifts his hands again.

'One last time,' I say, and fling him on the bed again. He bounces, sits up and crawls towards me. I lay on the bed.

He arrives beside me and climbs on my body. I hold him up in the air, his body horizontal to mine.

'Mummy and Daddy will be christening this bed soon,' I tell him.

He cackles loudly.

'I know. Wouldn't that be nice, huh?'

My mobile rings.

'Where are you?'

'In the master bedroom.'

'Don't move.'

We spend an hour together, playing, just as an ordinary family would. When Sorab nods off, we lay for a while with him between us, just looking into each other's eyes.

'We are so lucky, aren't we?' I whisper.

'I can hardly believe I have both of you.'

I grin. 'Wanna have sex?'

His answering grin is wolfish. 'Obviously.'

116

'What about His Highness?' I jerk my head in the direction of the sleeping child.

'He can have the bed,' he says, and grabbing my hand he slides me off the round bed. And there on the soft white carpet we have quiet sex. It is unfamiliar and in a funny way taboo, and so incredibly exciting.

When we finish I am giggling breathlessly. 'My knees,' I complain.

'We'll use the bed on the return trip,' Blake promises.

I stare at him in wonder. His hair is falling down his forehead, his eyes are sparkling and he looks so young and carefree.

We are flown by helicopter to the roof of the iconic and awesomely beautiful Burj Al Arab, considered the best of the three seven star hotels in the world. As soon as we step out on to the green felt landing pad, waiters in tails and white gloves stand in a line to greet us with champagne and flowers.

There is no check-in and we are immediately charmed into the royal suite. Inside the opulence is shocking. Its luxury and excess are such that it is almost intimidating. There is a butler outside the door who knows us all by name which I frankly find unnerving! I feel as if I am an impostor. Surely only kings and emperors live with gold and gilt on every surface and leopard skin-covered empire chairs.

The royal suite has red silk walls. The entrance hall leads to a grand staircase that has elaborately patterned and carved gold and black banisters. It has a faux leopard skin runner carpet. Even Jerry raises her eyebrows and goes silent on me. When she disappears into her bedroom with Sorab I turn to Blake.

'Well, what do you think?' he asks.

'It's all rather...heroic.'

He grins. 'I'm glad it was you who said it and not me.'

We laugh. At that moment I am the happiest person on earth.

'Shall we check out the bedroom?'

'Shall we wait until it's dark?'

'Chicken,' he teases and taking my hand pulls me towards the bedroom.

We stand at the doorway.

The room is huge with a brightly patterned carpet, gilded furniture, patterned wallpaper and gilded mirrors. The four-poster bed is massive and set on a purple pedestal, with curtains around it. Over it is a domed canopy with a pleated silk interior. There is the impression of a tent, but also the wild excess of Versace.

We turn to look at each other.

'Heroic,' we blurt out at precisely the same time and laugh.

'How much does it cost?'

'More than a hero's ransom.'

I chuckle. 'Come on, let's check out the bathroom.

There: gold marble walls, cream marble columns, and blue-veined chocolate marble floors,

gilded mirrors, polished bronze tiles, gold taps and fittings, and Hermes toiletries.

'Looks like fun times ahead for you and me,' Blake says looking meaningfully at the round Jacuzzi bath.

I grin. 'A midnight bath?'

'Who am I to turn down such a beautiful woman?'

'I've never been in a Jacuzzi.'

'Eyes tell a story. Yours tell me to open your legs and devour you.' His voice is low and throbbing with passion.

I watch the heat come into his eyes, the dark hunger, and my stomach twists with excitement. 'I like the word excess. It has sex inside it,' I whisper.

We use the hotel's Ferrari. It is scarlet and roars like some great beast when Blake guns it. Dubai, it turns out, is littered with speed cameras and Blake makes everyone of them flash.

We eat at At.mosphere, the highest restaurant in the world, one hundred and twenty-three floors away from the ground. The views are breathtaking.

'I fancy getting legless,' I announce.

Blake raises his eyebrows, but does not say anything while I knock the cocktails back.

'You don't mind, do you?' I ask, already tipsy.

'No, not at all. I'm actually rather curious. I've never seen you drunk.'

I giggle like a schoolgirl and look at him from beneath my eyelashes.

'What?' he asks.

'It feels as if I've always known you, perhaps even in other lifetimes.'

'You know what you're like?' His voice is but a whisper.

I lean forward. 'Tell me.'

'You're like a force that swept into my life, cast me into the winds, and set me ablaze. Afterwards you made me rise from the ashes, like a phoenix reborn.'

'Wow! That's deep.' I wave a finger towards the glass walls at the sky. 'And there you are flying in the skies.'

'I like drunk Lana.'

'Ooo... Is it already time for dessert?'

What looks like a chocolate ball arrives. I lift my eyes towards Blake.

'Want to taste?'

He shakes his head. 'Enjoy yourself.'

I tuck in. Delicious.

At the 'floating' staircase, going down, I become suddenly nervous. Blake kneels at my feet and takes my shoes off for me. Holding me tight we go down it. In the high-speed lift I start to feel a bit sick, but outside with cool breezes blowing on the fountain terrace, I recover very quickly and start to look forward to the Jacuzzi.

Blake looks at his watch, 'Come on,' he says and takes me closer to the water's edge. Suddenly music fills the air. I look around surprised. It is Pink and Nat Ruess.

'They're playing our song, Lana.'

I gaze up at him. 'You remembered.'

'How could I forget? The night is branded in my mind forever. You were so, so innocent and so very beautiful.' He puts his hands on either side of my cheeks and turns my face towards the fountains. 'Watch the fountains dance,' he says, and stands so close behind me.

I lean back and stare with amazement. All around me people are taking their phones out to record the stupendous spectacle. Indeed, they are dancing fountains. Soaring, leaning, bending, running like fire upon the surface of the water, all in tempo with the music. It is very beautiful and I am so overcome with joy that tears gather in my eyes and streak down my face.

When the last fountain dies down, he turns me around to face him.

'Why are you crying?'

I sniff loudly. 'These are happy tears. Just ignore me.'

'Until I met you I never wanted a woman's tears, but I want yours. I want your sighs, I want your laughter, I want your joy, your smell, your smile. I want it all.'

Behind me I hear fireworks. I turn my face up to the skies and watch the beautiful display. They are still exploding around us when Blake takes a ring out of his jacket and slips it on my finger.

I gaze down at it. It is the biggest pink diamond I have ever seen. It would have been gaudy if not for the plain setting and the astonishing intensity of its color. The light from the fireworks makes it glitter like a pink fire. It is also a perfect fit. It is too big and beautiful to not be... Is it? Could it really be? I look up at him with shocked eyes. The flare from the fireworks streak across his face.

'Are you asking me to marry you?'

'Nope.'

'Oh.' The wind changes. A fine mist of water from the fountain reaches us, lands on my skin. It is deliciously cool on my flushed skin.

'If you ask you might get a no and I'm not taking no for an answer. I'm telling you: we're getting married.'

For a moment I take in the beautiful, beautiful eyes, that tough, unyielding jaw, the straight mouth, the aristocratic nose, then I fling my arms around his neck and our lips meet in the most beautiful kiss. It is deep and lusty and romantic and just perfect. I forget the fireworks, the people, the fountain.

All I know is when he first kissed me a lifetime ago, he didn't kiss my lips, he kissed my soul.

Hey Beautiful,

Thank you! You've kept me this company this far into Blake and Lana's journey, and it will be my greatest pleasure to have you around until the series is complete.

The next part, Seduce Me, is told through the point of view of Lana's bridesmaid, Julie Sugar. It will be the conclusion of the Lana and Blake saga, but it is also the story of Julie's search for true love.

See you between the sheets of Seduce Me...

xx *Georgia*

https://www.facebook.com/georgia.lecarre

https://twitter.com/georgiaLeCarre

http://www.goodreads.com/GeorgiaLeCarre

Bonus Material

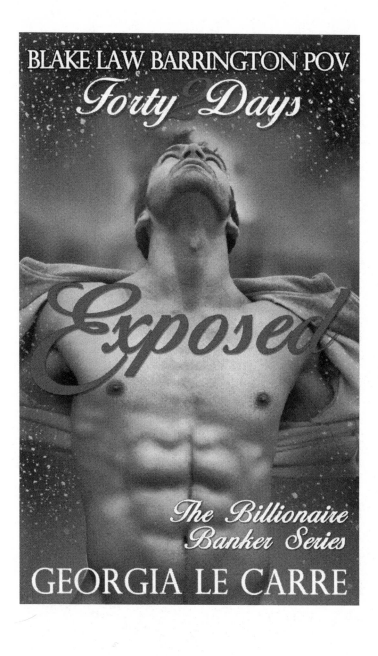

BLAKE LAW BARRINGTON POV

Forty & Days

Exposed

The Billionaire Banker Series

GEORGIA LE CARRE

POV
Forty 2 Days

When Blake Met Lana At the Bank

Chapter 1

For a whole fucking year I hear nothing.

She flies out of Heathrow with her mother, lands in Tehran and then... The trail goes stone cold. That still shocks me. The ease with which a woman can enter Iran, don a drab, loose-fitting garment, and simply disappear, become totally invisible. Without the powerful tentacles of a central bank in that country I have no way of tracking her financially either. The only connection left was the Swiss bank account, but that registered no activity, until recently, when the account was emptied and closed on the same day.

Then there was nothing left of her, but memories and hurt. Hurt like I had never imagined possible.

Sometimes, especially in the beginning when I didn't yet hate her, I used to imagine her veiled and in the desert. She always wanted to go there. My dreams were romantic then. Telescoped

126

without reality or reason we traveled in slow motion upon shifting sands, untroubled by the blazing sun, sharing a camel, only one goatskin water bag between us. In my dreams everything was perfect: the rocking of the camel, perfect. Her, perfect. Us, perfect.

And then I would wake up and feel like shit.

In the day I throw myself into work. At night I trawl the city's night scene looking for the same thing anyone who crawls into the underbelly of cities finds—moments of forgetfulness between the legs of strangers. But nothing would fill the void or the terrible longing for her.

I wanted us on one camel.

In my recurring fantasy, she comes to my office, talks her away around Laura, and opens my door. I am too shocked to stand. She comes towards me hips swaying, a slut. Dressed as I had found her that first night we met, she comes around the desk, swipes all my papers to the floor and sits on the table facing me. With one shoe she pushes my chair a little away. Then she lifts her legs, knees together, the way a girl who has been to finishing school is supposed to get out of a car, and pushes her butt deeper into the desk. I look at her. Her gaze is greedy, the way I know her eyes can be. She leans back so that both the palms of her hands are on the desk behind her, and spreads her legs wide open. My eyes slip down. There it is. Open: running with sweet juices.

'Get your mouth on it,' her red lips command. 'I've been dying for a good suck.'

But it is absolutely true what the philosophers say: love and hate are just two ends of the same string. You love someone, they lie to you, and you love them less; then they cheat on you, and you love them even less, and you keep going down that string until you hate them. So I traveled down that string.

I hate that woman, that is as obvious as hell to me, but it is also as clear as day that I cannot let her go. She cheated me. Kicked me when I was down. Brought me to my knees. No one has ever done that. Ever. If I do not punish her... Betrayal then, forever. I will know myself to be a weak man pretending to be strong. I must have my pound of flesh.

Then three days ago a little light on my computer screen flashed. For a moment my mind went blank. Then hot blood began to pulse again in my veins and my cheek muscles moved, my lips curved. I was smiling again.

'Gotcha.'

I hear footsteps approaching in the corridor and my heart begins to race. The excitement of seeing her again is so uncontrollably strong that it startles me. But I hate her guts. Immensely. This is purely about revenge. This is about me getting what I am owed. I lay my palms flat on the desk. I want to be cold and controlled. I don't want the bitch to have the satisfaction of knowing that she has affected me at all. The footsteps pause outside the door. I take a deep breath. She is nothing, I tell myself. She just wanted to count my money.

My face becomes an unfeeling mask.

I cease my wild thoughts.

A brief knock, and the door opens.

And... All the ugly words that had kept me sane—whore, slut, gold-digger, bitch—become empty balloons that are floating away. I cannot keep a single one. She may be a whore, a slut and a gold-digger, but she is mine. My slut, my bitch, my gold-digger.

Fuck, already I am itching to see her naked. I want to strip off that ugly suit she's wearing, pop her on the table and fuck her until she screams. That's the second part of the fantasy.

She walked in with a smile—big, false, irritating. That hurt. Obviously, she has not suffered as I have. Fortunately for her, the smile doesn't last long. Dies on contact with my person. Her face drains of color and her mouth hangs open. That's more like it, darling. Papa's here to get back what he is owed. You forgot—nobody cheats Papa. While she is doing a better than average impression of a goldfish, I study her. How thin she has become. Starving-African-children thin. Nobody should be that thin.

The employee who showed her in closes the door. Time to take control.

'Hello, Lana,' I say, remaining seated behind the desk. My voice comes out... Good. Encouraged, I add more words. 'Have a seat,' I invite. That, too, I am pleased to note, comes out smooth.

But she does not move. She keeps doing the goldfish thing, but doesn't find her voice. I see her swallow and try again.

'What are you doing here?' It is barely a hoarse whisper.

'Processing your loan application.'

She frowns. 'What?'

'I'm here to process your loan application,' I repeat with deliberate patience. I am enjoying this head fuck. The element of surprise has completely worked in my favor.

She shakes her head. 'You don't work here. You don't process tiny little loans.'

'I'm here to process yours.'

'Why?' Some thought crosses her mind and she is suddenly galvanized into action. 'So you can turn me down? Don't bother. I'll show myself out,' she cries hotly and begins to turn.

I am on my feet instantly, the chair wheeling away behind me. 'Lana, wait.'

She hesitates, looks up at me blankly.

'I am the one in the entire banking industry most likely to extend you this loan.'

She continues to stare at me.

'Please,' I continue, more carefully this time, 'take a seat.'

Dazed she looks at the two chairs facing me, but she does not move. 'How did you know I would be here today?

I tell her about the nifty little software that flags her name and date of birth if it comes up in the banking system.

 130

She frowns, but says nothing.

I need to engage with her. The shock has dazed her. 'Is all the money in the Swiss account gone?'

She nods distractedly. 'But why are you here?'

'Same reason as before.'

'For sex.'

I sort of lose my head then. 'Sex?' I hiss, my jaw clenching tight. 'God, you have no idea, have you?' I go around the table and advance towards her. Honestly, at that moment I want to throttle her. How easily she had said that word, diminished all my intolerable pain and my insatiable longing into one meaningless action. She carries on staring at me, almost fearfully. I stop a foot in front of her, electricity crackling between us. I take one more step and we are inches apart and suddenly I smell her. I breathe in the scent. *What the...?*

Baby powder!

Sick, but it fires up my imagination the way the most expensive perfume cannot. Like a snake, lust is uncoiling in the pit of my belly, spitting its venom into my veins. I want her so bad I ache. Quickly, I lower my eyelids, but it is as if she has already seen the potency of my desire for her. For the first time since she came into the room, color tinges her skin.

She reaches out a trembling hand toward me.

My reaction is instant and beyond my control. 'Don't,' I rasp, stiffening. I cannot let her have the upper hand. This has to be all my way. And there is no highway for this little bird.

Shocked by the violence of my reaction, she retracts her hand. I see the realization in her eyes. Now she knows she has damaged me. Her face crumples as if she gives a flying fuck. What an actress.

'Please,' she whispers.

She put a lot emotion into that word and I am shocked at how much I want to believe that it is not an act. My pathetic neediness annoys me. I bend my head toward her face. Her eyes are riveted on my lips. What is she remembering? The taste of me?

'Dishonest little Lana,' I murmur, so close to her neck that if I put my tongue out I'd lick that tender skin. I run my hand down the smoothness of her neck—skin like pure silk. I let my fingers wrap around it—so slender, so breakable. I hear her draw in a sharp breath. Languidly I slip my hand into the collar of her cheap blouse.

She begins to tremble. I pay no attention. Instead I watch my fingers slip a button out of its hole and then another. I spread apart the joined material so that her throat, chest, and the lacy tops of her bra are exposed. The desire to rip her clothes is so strong I have to physically fight it. I frown. Yes, she is very beautiful, but I have had other very beautiful women—why does this woman alone have such an effect on me? Even knowing what I know about her doesn't change a thing. Not having total control over my own impulses makes me feel vulnerable and defenseless. It is like falling backwards into nothing. I hate the sensation. I can never let her see my weakness. I turn coldly furious. The breaths that escape her lips are suddenly shallow and quick. I smile possessively. So nothing has changed on that front.

'You were, by far, more when you squeezed into that little orange dress and your fuck me shoes, and went looking for money,' I taunt. 'Look at you now; you're flapping around inside a man's jacket. Two hundred thousand and you don't even buy yourself a nice suit.'

I tut. 'And this...' I raise my hand to her hair. 'This ugly bun. What were you thinking of?' I ask softly, as I pluck the pins out of her hair and drop them on the ground. I return her hair to its silk curtain. Beautiful. I reach back, pull a tissue out of its box and start wiping away her lipstick, a horrid plum. I am unhurried—let her stew from the outside in.

I toss the stained tissue on the ground. 'That's better.'

She stares at me helplessly, and guess what? It turns me on to have her at my mercy.

'Lick your lips,' I order.

'What?' She looks horrified by the cold command, and yet electrified by the sexual heat that my order obviously arouses. Like a beautifully tuned guitar, the tension in her body matches mine. I feel the same desire rippling through her.

We have played this game before. We both know where it leads.

My jaw hardens. 'You heard me.'

The tip of her small, pink tongue protrudes and I eye its sweet journey avidly. 'That's more like it. That's the mercenary bitch I know,' I say, thrusting a rough hand into her hair. It is exactly as I remember it. Soft and silky. A year of waiting. Bitch! I tug and pull her head back. She gasps with shock, but her eyes are wide, unafraid, and innocent. Fuck you, Lana. You're no innocent. We had a deal and you cheated me. And that fucking Dear John letter? You didn't even have the decency to wait until I got out of hospital. I could have been dead for all she cared. I expect better from a two bit whore. But the thing that hurt the most: she didn't care.

Now I will have my revenge. Another part of my brain is sneering—you're fighting a losing battle here, dude.

The thought powers me to kiss her. This kiss means nothing to me. It is only a way of gauging her reaction. I will not allow myself to get sucked into it. I descend on her roughly, painfully, violently, purposely bruising her soft lips, my mouth so savage that she utters a strangled, soundless cry. That sound wakes up an uncivilized beast. I make room for it. The intense desire to hurt and have my revenge is greater than me. Let her understand that I am not the same man that I was then. Before she betrayed me.

I taste the fury in my kiss: blood!

Really, Blake? But I cannot stop. Cannot control my emotions. Cannot resist her. Cannot live without her. I don't allow myself to feel.

A moan escapes her. And it affects me—in a way I could never have guessed. It almost makes me forget my carefully laid plans. It almost makes me take her on the floor of this drab office. The effect this woman has on me is incredible. I feel raw and starved. No matter what she does or what she is, I want her. All I want is to be buried deep inside her, but I am not a Barrington for nothing. Years of iron control come to my rescue. One of us is going to get hurt this time, and it will not be me.

Her hands reach up to push me away, but her palms meet the solidity of my chest, and as if with minds of their own, they push aside the lapels of my jacket, and her fingers splay open on my shirt. Oh, I know that sign. Pure submission. She's mine. I can do anything with her now. But I want more, more than just sexual surrender. I've got a plan. And I'm sticking to it.

I change the kiss, gentle it. Instantly her body scents victory and tries to burrow closer to me, but I keep my grip on her hair, relentless and tinged with hurting force. I cannot let her get nearer. I am in dangerous territory. One wrong move and I will fall into her honey trap again. She tries pushing her hips toward my crotch. Can't have that. That would give me away.

I end the kiss nonchalantly, as if I have just participated in a meaningless encounter, or a polite social interaction. With the same feigned lack of emotion I put her away and casually prop myself against the desk. I fold my arms across my chest, and watch her with great satisfaction. This is my territory. Here I am boss. This time, Lana honey...

She stands before me aroused, breasts heaving and hands clenched at her sides as she tries to regain some measure of composure.

I smile. Round one—me.

Silently she takes two steps forward, reaches a hand out and puts a finger on my throat. I freeze. I can feel her skin on my frantically beating pulse. And just like that we are connected. We never break eye contact. Fuck her.

Round two—is not over yet.

'Is it sex when I want to see you come apart?' I ask bitterly.

Her face crumples. This woman deserves an Oscar. She takes her finger away from my throat. 'What do you want, Blake?'

'I want you to finish your contract.'

She drops her face into her hands. 'I can't,' she whispers.

'Why not? Because you took the money and ran while I lay in a hospital bed?'

She takes a deep breath, but does not look up. Guilty as charged.

'I was cut up to start with,' I say as coldly as I can. I don't want to give her any more power than she already holds.

She looks up. Butter wouldn't melt in that sweet O. 'You were cut up?'

'Funny thing that, but yes.'

'I thought it was just a sex thing for you,' she murmurs.

'If you wanted money why didn't you ask me?' My voice is harsh.

'I...' She shakes her head.

'You made a serious miscalculation, didn't you, Lana, my love? The honey pot is here.' I pat the middle of my chest.

She simply gazes at my hand.

'But not to worry,' I say sarcastically. 'All is not lost. There's money in the pot.'

How predictable. Her gaze lifts up to my mouth.

'You did me a favor.' I try to sound detached, but my voice comes out bitter and pained. 'You opened my eyes. I see you now for what you were... Are. I was blinded by you. I made the classic mistake. I fell in love with an illusion of purity.'

She carries on looking at me blankly.

'If I had not bought you that night you would have gone with anyone, wouldn't you? You are not admirable. You are despicable.'

'So why do you want me to finish the contract?' she asks breathily.

'I am like the drug addict who knows his drug is poison. He despises it, but he cannot help himself. So that we are totally clear—I *detest* myself. I am ashamed of my need for you.'

'The... The...people who paid me—'

'They can do nothing to you. My family—'

She interrupts. 'What about Victoria?'

And suddenly I feel very angry. What the fuck has Victoria to do with this? This is between me and her. Besides, I am fond of Victoria and hide a measure of guilt for the pain I have caused her. Her shock when I tried to break off our engagement surprised me. I had imagined that she was marrying me for the same reasons I was—consolidation, security, and continuity—but in fact she is in love with me. If anything, the extent of her possessive passion worried me a little. A marriage of convenience only works when both parties exhibit similar detachment. I don't want to think of it now, but the truth is that I do not want Victoria. At that moment I realize that I can never marry Victoria. But for now I will deal with the most pressing problem I have: I cannot think of being with anyone other than the witch standing in front of me.

Angrily I forbid her to ever again drag Victoria into our arrangement. A flash goes off in her eyes. It's gone in a second, but even lidded it reeks of jealousy! I seize the opportunity to manipulate her by exaggerating Victoria's loyalty. I rub it in that Victoria stood by me through my worst period while she swanned off to Iran. 'One day,' I tell her, 'I will wake up and this sickness will be gone. Until then... You owe me forty-two days, Lana.'

She closes her eyes and hangs her head.

'Name your price,' I demand curtly.

Her head snaps up. 'No.' Her voice is very strong and sure. 'You don't have to pay me again. I will finish the contract.'

'Good,' I remark casually, but I turn away from her immediately. Cannot let her see how elated I am by her capitulation. I can hardly believe I have

won so easily. My mind is doing victory back-flips as I go around the desk, and retake my position behind it.

Chapter 2

I slide into the black swivel chair and open the file in front of me. 'So, you're setting up a business?'

She drops into one of the chairs opposite me and tells me that she and Billie are thinking of starting a business. I ask the appropriate questions but my mind is elsewhere. I am not interested in hearing about her business plans.

'That reminds me, how is your mother?'

To my surprise her face contorts with pain. Seconds pass in acute silence. 'She passed away.'

I lean forward, eyes narrowed, shocked. 'I thought the treatment was working.'

She bites the words out. 'A car. Hit and run.'

'I'm sorry. I'm real sorry to hear that, Lana.' And I am, too, really sorry. She was a good woman. I liked her.

She blinks fast. Oh my God, she is going to burst into tears. She stands. I stand, too. Immediately she puts out a hand to ward me off, and runs to the door. In an instant I don't hate her anymore; all my desire to hurt crumbles to dust and I just want to help her, make it easier, take her in my arms and protect her. I stride toward her and grab her arm. She twists away from me, but my grip is too firm.

'This way. There's a staff restroom,' I say quietly, and quickly opening the door I lead her

down the corridor. From the corners of my eyes I can see the tears are streaming down her cheeks. I hold open the toilet door and she rushes in. The door swings closed in my face.

I stand there looking at the door and then I hear her. Wailing for her mother. I lift my hand to push the door open, but I don't. I take a step back. Then I begin to pace. I have never heard anyone cry like that. I come from a family where all our expressions of sorrow are carefully controlled, a dab from a handkerchief to the eye. When my grandfather died, my grandmother did not even stop the journey of her cup to her mouth. Only after she had swallowed her sip of tea did she say, 'Oh dear.' At the funeral not a tear was shed, by anybody.

More than once I go to the door and almost push it open. I want to go in, but I cannot. My feet refuse to move forward. Anyway, it is clear that she does not want me, and that it is unsafe for me. I am already too confused and unhinged by a few minutes in her company. A woman appears in the corridor apparently heading for the toilet. She glances at me and I growl at her. Yeah, that's right, I growl.

She does a hundred and eighty degree right turn and flees. I look at my watch. Five minutes have passed. The wailing has become long sobs. I continue to pace. I jam my fists into the pockets of my trousers. She'll be out soon. Suddenly the sobs stop. I go to the door. The door is cheap and I hear the tap running. I step away instantly and move a few feet away from it. I lean my back against the wall and stare at the ground. For the last year I have been dead inside. Now all kinds of thoughts, desires, and emotions are coming to the fore. They are like those strange, mud-covered creatures that the tide uncovers when it goes back to sea. The door opens. She is standing there, her blouse buttoned to the neck. She won't lift her eyes. She won't meet mine.

'Are you okay?'

She nods.

'Tom will take you home.'

Very slowly her eyes, the eyelashes damp and sticking together, rise up to meet mine. They are like her voice. Level. There is nothing there to hold on to. 'No,' she says. 'Let's get this loan business out of the way.'

If she had slapped me in the face it would have been better.

We go back to the clinical office.

I take up my position behind the desk once more. 'Baby Sorab?' I say and look up from her application form.

And what I see chills my blood. Her face is cold and totally devoid of expression. How could she howl one moment for her mother then sit opposite me with that look. She shrugs carelessly.

'Yes. We thought it was a good name for our business.'

'Why baby clothes?' It seems a curious business for two young girls to get into.

'Billie has always been good with colors. She can put red and pink together and make them look divine. And since Billie had her baby this year we decided to make baby clothes?'

'Billie had a baby?' I frown. I thought she was a lesbian. And then it hits me, of course. It's what they do. Have a baby—the government gives them a flat and an income for the next eighteen years!

'Yeah, a beautiful boy,' she says, and suddenly I have a gut feeling. She's lying about something. She says something else and I reply, but it is all just a charade. One I lose interest in prolonging.

'OK,' I say.

'OK what?'

'OK you got the loan.'

'Just like that?'

'There is one condition.'

She becomes very still.

'You do not get the money for the next forty-two days.'

'Why?'

'Because,' I say softly, 'for the next forty-two days you will exist only for my pleasure. I plan to gorge on your body until I am sick to my stomach.'

'Are you going to house me in some apartment again?'

'Not *some* apartment—the same one as before.'

She sits up straighter. She looks me in the eye. She has some stipulations, too. She wants to bring Billie's baby to the apartment for four nights a week. And she wants Billie and Jack—the guy she thinks of as her brother and I fucking know is in love with her—to be allowed to come to the apartment. I don't like the idea, but I let it go for now. Nothing she has asked for is what I would consider a deal breaker. The baby might be annoying, but I'm cool with Billie. Jack might be another matter but I will handle that with time.

I engineer a bored expression. 'Anything else?'

'No.'

'Fine. Have you plans for tomorrow?'

She shakes her head.

'Good. Keep tomorrow free. Laura will call you to go through the necessary arrangements.'

'OK. If there is nothing else...'

'I'll walk you out.'

Heads turn to watch us. I ignore them all, but Lana seems disturbed by their regard. Again I have that unfamiliar sensation of wanting to protect and shield her. The bank manager catches sight of us and hurries toward me. He has an odd expression on his face, a cross between constipated and stricken, no doubt horribly concerned that I could leave without giving him the chance to flatter me. I lift a finger and he stops abruptly. I pull open the heavy door and we go into the late summer air. It is wet and gray, but it is not cold.

In the drizzle we face each other and make small talk. Suddenly the chitchat dries up in my throat and we are eating each other. The blue of her eyes reaches right up into my body and tears at my soul like a hungry hawk. Its power is enormous. In its claws I feel myself losing my grip.

144

A gust of wind lifts my hair and deposits it on my forehead. She puts a hand out to touch it, but I jerk back. I won't be won over so easily.

'This time you won't fool me,' I say harshly.

We stare at each other. She astonished, and me, contemptuously. Her hand drops limply to her side. Suddenly she looks unbearably young and exhausted. She glances down the road at the bus stand.

'I'll see you tomorrow then.' In the bustle of the street her voice is barely audible.

'Tom's here,' I say, as the Bentley pulls up along the curb.

She shakes her head. 'Thanks, but I'll take the bus.'

'Tom will drop you off,' I insist.

'Fuck you,' she snaps suddenly. 'Our contract doesn't start until tomorrow. So today I'll decide my mode of transport.' She swings away from me.

My hand shoots out and grasps her wrist. 'I will pick you up and put you in that car if necessary. You decide.'

'Oh, yeah? And I'll call the police.'

I laugh. 'After everything I've told you about the system—that's your answer?'

She sags. All the fight gone out of her. 'Of course, who will believe me if I claim that a Barrington tried to force me to take a lift?' She resorts to begging. 'Please, Blake.'

This one is non-negotiable. There is no way that she is taking the bus. I know how to stop her in her

tracks. 'Very well, Tom will go with you on the bus.'

At that point she stops arguing, simply turns around, opens the car door, gets in, slams it shut, and stares straight ahead.

Tom turns around and says something to her and she answers as the vehicle pulls away.

I stand on the sidewalk looking at the car, willing her to turn and look back. Now, Lana, now. If she turns before the car disappears out of sight it will all be all right. Turn, Lana. Please turn back. Turn back and look at me. As the car turns at the traffic light she twists her neck and looks at me. Her face is white and expressionless. But inside me wild joy surges. I want to punch the air. Never have I experienced such a strong current of emotion in my body.

Then the oddest thing happens.

Perhaps it is the churn of high emotions that I almost never allow myself to indulge in, or perhaps it is the shock of seeing her again, but I am no longer standing on Kilburn High Street with badly dressed strangers shuffling around me.

I am five years old and alone and terrified in a room lit only by a naked light blub. I look down at my hands and they are covered in blood. My shirt, my shorts, my legs, even the floor around me has turned red. The blood is not fresh: my fingers are stuck to the knife. The knife is not mine. The blood is not mine. I rip the knife from my hand and let it clatter on the floor noisily. I pull my eyes away

from the glinting blade, and thought I don't want to, I let them travel along the cement floor. Until…

I come upon what I have done.

I did that!

No. It cannot be.

I open my mouth and scream for my Mommy, but no sound will come out. I scream and scream, but no one comes. No one can hear me.

No one.

POV
Forty 2 Days

When Blake Met Sorab

I paused at the bathroom door, shocked.

She was laughing, I mean really laughing, the way I had never seen her do while with me. The laughter was like a fountain of fresh, sweet water bubbling up from deep inside her being. I stared at her as if I was a man who had been wandering in a desert for days without food or water.

I don't know how long I stood there simply staring. At the sight of water. So near and yet so far away. You're no better than a heroin addict desperate for his next fix, a voice inside my head taunted. But at that moment there was nothing, nothing I wanted more than to take her in my arms and never ever let her go again.

What was it about this woman that made her impossible to resist even when it was patently clear I shouldn't trust her further than I could throw her? Slowly, as if in a dream, I was drawn to the centre of her attention—to the shrieking, splashing, lustily laughing baby. It was obvious.

She loved that little creature.

Instantly, I was jealous of it, of the love she had for it. The jealousy didn't strike me like a bolt, more like weevils crawling all over me. The feeling disgusted me. I didn't want to be jealous of a fucking baby. I wanted to hate her guts. A small sound came from my throat.

I didn't plan it: it was involuntary.

Her head whirled around, and right before my eyes, quite interesting really, I watched her withdraw, build a wall around herself. And I had to stop myself from laughing in her face. She knew me so little. Did she really think I was going to hit that wall, and just stop? No wall could keep me out. I would scale it, brick by fucking brick. Nothing, no one could keep me out.

Until I said so she was mine. To do with as I pleased.

'Hi,' she fluttered, nervous, very nervous. And so she should be. A secret thrill fizzled in my veins. I wanted to throttle her. Little bitch. How dare she love the kid and not me?

'Who do we have here?' I said softly, going into the room.

I looked into the child's big, blue eyes—solemn, curious, unafraid—and suddenly, that disassociated, unreal feeling I hadn't felt since I was child drifted in. My mind didn't say, 'Who are you?' It said, 'Who am I?' I felt like one of those turtles in Asia that have had their throats slit while still alive and I was bleeding out to make a blood cocktail for some demented human.

Something was wrong with the picture I was looking at. My mind began to race. The baby grinned toothlessly, and in that instant, I understood everything. The slit in my throat healed itself. The incessant feeling of being empty and lost receded.

That was *my son* in my tub. And that was *my* woman standing beside him.

In that same moment of illumination I felt the danger. It was in the room standing beside me, like an invisible shadow. But by the time I turned to look at her, my eyes were neutral, betraying nothing. We looked at each other.

I saw the fear, but I also saw the love in her eyes. How could I have missed it? I felt rage, murderous rage at what had been done to her, to us, but also wild and leaping joy that she loved me. That she was pure. She had acted as a mother. Only as a mother. I wanted to grab her and kiss her.

'Does he cry a lot?' I asked finally, my voice so smooth and normal even I was impressed.

'No. Most nights he will sleep right through,' she assured quickly.

I saw the relief in her face. I marveled at that. She must think me a fool. It would work in my favor.

'Good,' I said with a nod, and as if losing interest, I turned away and went out.

My legs took me to the dining room. I closed the door, leaned back against it, and closed my eyes. When I opened my eyes I knew what I must do. I knew, too that this apartment was no longer safe for my family, but moving them would alert him. The only thing in my favor was stealth. As long as he thought I didn't know I could lay my plans. Otherwise, he would win. He had nothing to lose, and I everything. I picked up the phone and called a business associate. I talked business for twelve minutes. My voice betrayed nothing.

I opened my briefcase. Took some papers out. Looked them over carefully. Made notes on them. Left messages for Laura to action in the morning. But all the time the best and most efficient part of me was coldly, meticulously planning the future. Hours later, I went into the bedroom. I knew he was listening and watching. Let him listen. Let him watch. He would hear and see nothing different. I closed the door softly. She was already in bed, and by the sound of her even breathing, asleep.

Quietly, I stepped through the connecting door that had been left ajar. A sliver of light came in from the door leading into the corridor. I walked up to the cot and stood over him. I was surprised at the rush of pride that coursed through my body at the sight of his sleeping body. I stood in the dark and fought the intense longing to feel the texture of his skin. I clenched my fists.

Soon, soon I would claim him as mine, but not now.

Tomorrow, when it wouldn't appear 'strange' I would touch him. I listened to my body, to the whisper of the purest emotion I had ever experienced. To love without expecting anything in return. With it came the instinct to protect what was mine. They will not do to him what they did me and Marcus. Without another glance at him I left as quietly as I had entered.

I sat next to her and she opened her eyes sleepily. My beauty. I loved her more than life itself. I would kill with my bare hands for her. I bent my head and kissed her. The kiss was gentle and soft. She came awake and opened her mouth. The kiss deepened. That raw hunger between us throbbed into life.

So: he wanted to watch me with my woman. Let him. Watch while you can, Daddy. I know what you are capable of, but you don't know what I am capable of. I slid my hand down her silky body and tugged at the rim of her knickers. I laid my fingers flat between her legs. Dampness seeped out from under the material.

'You are so wet,' I whispered, and inserted a finger into her.

She tensed.

Immediately I stilled. 'What's the matter?'

'Nothing,' she mumbled. I put my hand out and flicked on the light switch. She blinked and squinted.

I lifted her gown up and turned her over. What I saw cut me to shreds. I wanted to cry. I did that to her!

POV
The Billionaire Banker

When Blake Saw Rupert Mauling Lana At The Party

The brute had her pinned against a wall, his big body completely hiding her from my view. Must have only been minutes, but it was like a lifetime watching that broad back and thick neck. I had to fight the instinct to go over. Break them up. But I am a strategist, a man who knows when to pounce, how to exploit an opportunity. Not yet. Soon. Lose a battle to win the war. So I clenched my teeth and waited.

A woman came and wrapped herself around me. She laid her perfectly manicured red fingernails on the lapels of my jacket and smiled slyly. I glanced down at her and shuddered. I hate it when women I don't fancy throw themselves at me. At that precise moment Lothian moved his thick body away and I saw Lana. Flattened against the wall, her face white, mascara streaking down her face, and her lips already beginning to swell.
Our eyes met.

Fuck me, I looked into her shocked, defenseless eyes, and I did not feel lust! I did not want to take and use and discard as I had done with all the others. The only thing I registered in my body was the unfamiliar need to protect. Not myself but her. That same sensation I had experienced once a long time ago as a young boy, when I had come across an injured baby bird that had fallen out of its nest. I had scooped it in my cupped hands and warmed it inside my jacket. Taking it home I had made a nest for it and fed it warmed, sweet tea. After it died that evening, I had never again experienced that sensation. Until now.

Stunned by my own reaction I watched as she ran out of the room in her ridiculous shoes. And the dirty looks she got. You should have seen them. You'd have thought she stank of *their* bullshit. I despised my kind then.

In the corridor I saw her lurch unsteadily towards the powder room.

Less than a minute later I removed the red fingernails from my person, made my excuses and went to wait for her in the corridor. What the fuck was I doing? But the rational, thinking Blake had gone numb. And another part, a secret part of me, that I never let out, that I refused to even acknowledge, had come out and taken over. I crossed my arms and lounged against the wall.

When she came out, I almost did not recognize her. Underneath the layer of badly applied make-up she had the face of a schoolgirl. Hell, she had better not be under-aged. That would be all my plans down the toilet. I straightened and waited for her to come up to me. She was no longer crying. Her head was held high and those indescribably turquoise eyes were proud and flashing, and she would have walked right past me, too, if I had not raised a detaining finger.

An Interview With Blake Law Barrington

Q: What were you thinking or feeling when you approached Rupert Lothian's table where Lana was seated?

A: **Probably confidence. The plan was simple, guaranteed to succeed: When dealing with a psychopath always appeal to the narcissist in them. It doesn't work with sociopaths; they are a different species all together, but it never fails to fell the psychopath. Invite one to a party of his superiors and he will drop whatever plans he has to pander to his need to feel important.**

Obviously, once I got him and the girl at the party I would play it by ear. There has not been a woman yet that I wanted that I have not had, so I was pretty certain I was going to bed that girl.

However, what I heard as I walked to the table made me smile. It wasn't just going to easy. It was the proverbial candy from a baby scenario.

Q: Why were you so determined to bid for Lana?

A: **I told myself it was just sex, but** I should have known even then. Who was I kidding? Just sex? With her? That would *never* be enough. Some part of me must have recognised that this girl *was* the siren, the temptress that my father had warned me about. The one specially chosen to bring me to my knees. But at that moment I was the moth flying helplessly towards the flame. I guess, I just wanted her light, more than I wanted anything else...

Q: What went through your mind during that first kiss with Lana?
A: **Did you just ask me what went through my mind during that first kiss?**

Q: Yes. Some readers expressed an interest in your thoughts?
A: **Chuckles...Thoughts? My mind was blank. I'd never kissed any girl who made me respond the way her lips and body did. I had to struggle to stay normal.**

Q: Can you share with us your true feelings when you had sex for the first time?
A: **She'd pissed me off at the restaurant so I was determined not to go out of my way to be nice. I would simply treat her as one did a whore. I'd paid for her and we had an agreement and that was that. She'd said she didn't want it sweet and flowery, so I'd give it**

to her straight. But then I found out she was virgin and you know the rest...

Q: Do you remember your first impression of Lana's best friend, Billie?
A: I'd never actually met anyone like her, a woman with spider tattoos on her neck! Obviously, I've seen pictures of women like that, but I'd never met one in person. I was rather shocked though, by how level-headed she was...and her loyalty to Lana surprised and impressed me. She's unique.

Q: And what about how you felt when you were introduced to Jack?
A: Straight off I knew that he was in love with Lana and I remember that I didn't like it, but I also knew Lana held him in high esteem so I said nothing. Left it alone and waited to see what would develop.

Q: Could you describe for my readers what you felt when Lana arrived at Madame Yula?
A: The first time: pure excitement. Couldn't wait to undress her. And when she came wearing that electric blue blouse and those leather trousers, I experienced in my body the powerful sensation of ownership. That was the moment she became mine. And the more I tried to fight the feeling the more deeply I wanted her.

That night I wanted brand her, with my lips, my body, my dick. I wanted to come inside her.

Q: And the second time?
A: **Totally different. I was furious with her and I wanted my revenge, and yet even I knew it was more than that. Much more. As soon as she walked through the door, everyone else ceased to exist, I felt that invisible pull, and I all I wanted to do was grab her by the hair, drag her back to the apartment fuck her so hard walking was no longer an option.**

Q: What did you really feel the moment you discovered Lana was a virgin?
A: **Shock. I was shocked. I'd never been with a virgin. And when she cried...I was confused.**

Q: Confused?
A: **Yeah. I was overwhelmed by a strong totally foreign urge to hold and comfort her. And those kinds of emotions I didn't want or need. This was meant to be sex thing. Three months, maybe four, tops six. So wanting to hold on to someone you've paid money to use: warning bells were clanging in my head.**

Q: What was going through your head when you met Lana's mother?
A: **She was sweet and well educated and she obviously loved her daughter very much. I liked her and I was very sorry when I heard**

she died. Something brave about her. Lana has that same quality. I rate it very highly in a person.

Q: At what point did you realize your feelings had changed towards Lana?
A: **It happened almost immediately, but I was slow to recognize it, or more likely, I didn't want to recognize it.**

Q; The first morning, waking up together, what did you feel?
A: **The morning-after scene is always a bore, but seduced by the smell of her hair and the feel of her skin—he has the most amazing skin, like a baby soft and silky—I stayed.**

Q: What went through your head when Lana first declared her love to you?
A: **If someone takes money to leave you while you are lying unconsciousness in some hospital and afterwards never bothers to contact you again, what would you think if they then claimed to love you. What would you think? Exactly. I thought she was a fucking liar and I hated her guts, but still I wanted her.**

Q: Which emotion was stronger, anger or lust, when you met Lana again at the bank?
A: **To start with anger, somewhere in the middle of the encounter, lust. And then when she cried over her mother's death, tenderness,**

and then it was back to fury. And as she rose to leave, pure triumph. I got her...where I wanted her.

Q: How did you deal with having to choose Lana over his father?

A: **Sometimes I have nightmares. In it I am in the plane with my father. He is in his thirties. His hair is without grey and he is slim and tall. He is calmly eating chateaubriand with béarnaise sauce and chips.**

"You betrayed me," he says, wiping his mouth on a napkin. "The same fate awaits you."

And a hole appears in the side of the plane and he is sucked out. His expression is one of indescribable terror. "Your son will do to you what you have done to me."

And I wake up in a cold sweat.

Made in the USA
Lexington, KY
14 October 2016